P

Dr Mitch Reynolds finally found the cafeteria.

Kids dashed from one side of the room to the other among a sea of red, white and green balloons. The familiar pang of longing pierced his heart. He was turning away, intent on putting as much distance between himself and the painful reminder as he could, when he caught sight of a petite brunette, wearing a strange elf costume.

Arrested by the image, he froze. The woman was pretty, in spite of the green tights and tunic. What held his attention was the way she tended to the child, smoothing a hand over the girl's hair and smiling down at her with a caring, compassionate gaze. His gaze lingered on her legs—until he pulled himself together.

Enough. The cute elf wasn't his concern. In fact, if he were smart he'd stay far away from any hint of temptation...

Laura Iding loved reading as a child, and when she ran out of books she readily made up her own, completing a little detective mini-series when she was twelve. But, despite her aspirations for being an author, her parents insisted she look into a 'real' career. So the summer after she turned thirteen she volunteered as a Candy Striper and fell in love with nursing. Now, after twenty years of experience in trauma/critical care, she's thrilled to combine her career and her hobby into one—writing Medical Romances™ for Mills & Boon®. Laura lives in the northern part of the United States, and spends all her spare time with her two teenage kids (help!), a daughter and a son, and her husband. Enjoy!

Recent titles by the same author:

THE FLIGHT DOCTOR'S ENGAGEMENT*
THE CONSULTANT'S HOMECOMING
A PERFECT FATHER
THE FLIGHT DOCTOR'S EMERGENCY*

**Air Rescue*

THE DOCTOR'S CHRISTMAS PROPOSAL

BY

LAURA IDING

First published in Great Britain 2006
Harlequin Mills & Boon Limited,
Eton House, 18-24 Paradise Road, Richmond, Surrey TW9 1SR

ISBN-13: 978 0 263 84767 3
ISBN-10: 0 263 84767 5

Set in Times Roman 10½ on 13¼ pt
03-1106-44102

Printed and bound in Spain
by Litografia Rosés, S.A., Barcelona

THE DOCTOR'S CHRISTMAS PROPOSAL

To Mom and Dad I.

Thanks for all the wonderful Christmas
gatherings at the Iding house.

CHAPTER ONE

DANA WHITNEY HIKED her itchy neon-green tights up and tried not to grimace as the bells around her wrists and ankles tinkled merrily. So much for her attempt to get into the Christmas spirit. She felt ridiculous. None of the other ICU nurses were standing in the middle of Trinity Medical Center's cafeteria dressed as one of Santa's elves for the children's Christmas party. Why in the world had she thought this would be a good idea?

Because she'd made a promise to her mother before she'd died. Dana rolled her shoulders to ease the tension creeping along her neck accompanying the memories. Her promise to remember only the good times and not the sad times during the holidays was going to be harder to keep than she'd thought. Forcing off a wave of sorrow, she tugged on the green tunic that ended about mid-thigh and dodged a couple of kids running past her, chasing balloons.

Keeping busy would be the key. And reveling in the true meaning of Christmas. Not the easiest thing to do while dressed as an elf. Luckily she was scheduled to work over the holidays so she wouldn't be sitting home alone.

A little girl tugged on her tunic. Dana glanced down.

"Is it my turn yet?" the child asked.

Realizing she'd lost track for a moment, Dana flashed a guilty smile. "Yes. Here you go." Dana lifted the girl and sat her on Santa's lap.

"Ho, ho, ho. Merry Christmas!" Santa, who was currently being played by Dr. Joe Sansone gave a hearty chuckle. "So, little girl, what would you like Santa to bring you for Christmas?"

"You're not really Santa." The little girl stared at him with wide, serious blue eyes. "Are you?"

"Well, now, you're smart to figure out Santa is up at the North Pole, hard at work in his toy shop." Joe winked at the girl. "But he needs helpers like me so that we can keep track of what each child wants for Christmas. What's your name, honey?"

"Wendy Kinkade. I'm seven."

Santa nodded. "And I'll bet you've been a very good girl this year, too. What would you like for Christmas, Wendy?"

"New lungs for my mommy."

Huh? Dana wondered if she'd misunderstood but, no, Wendy's earnest gaze never wavered from Santa's face.

"New lungs for your mommy?" Joe caught Dana's gaze and lifted a questioning brow.

Dana gave a helpless shrug and swept a glance around the area. Sure enough, there was a woman wearing oxygen seated in a wheelchair off to the side of the group of rambunctious kids. In addition to appearing pale and drawn, the woman looked familiar. Dana wrinkled her brow, trying to place her.

"Yes." Wendy bobbed her head. "My mommy's on the transplant list, but we've been waiting a really, really long time."

"I see." Santa cleared his throat, and Dana suspected Joe was hesitant to promise something that would likely take a medical miracle. Of all the various transplant lists, waiting for lungs took the longest. A wave of compassion swept over her.

"Please? I know it's asking for a lot, but I don't need any toys and neither does my brother, Chad."

"Come on, Wen." Her brother rolled his eyes and looked around as if embarrassed. "Hurry up already."

"I promise to pass your request on to Santa, but he can't make new lungs in his toy shop," Joe cautioned.

"I know. But Santa is magic, so I'm sure he can get my mommy a new set of lungs without having to make them." Wendy smiled, revealing a gap from her missing front tooth. "Thanks, Mr. Santa's helper."

Chad walked up to lift his sister down from Santa's lap then turned away, obviously too grown-up to take his turn on Santa's lap. "Geez, Wen. I can't believe you didn't ask for the latest Glo-doll or a new bike. Santa's not going to be able to help Mom move up on the transplant list." With a snort of disgust, he reached for her hand. "Let's go. Mom's waiting."

"Wait. Don't forget your gift." Dana pulled herself together long enough to grab a gift stocking out of her bag for Wendy. "Do you want one, too, Chad? There's candy inside."

The boy looked as if he might refuse then gave a jerky nod. "Thanks," he muttered when she handed him another stocking. He tugged on his sister's hand, steering her through the crowd to where the woman in the wheelchair waited patiently. Finally her memory clicked.

"Jessica Kinkade." Dana snapped her fingers as she recognized the patient who'd been admitted off and on to the ICU. Dana looked at Joe. "Wendy's mother has pulmonary hypertension. She's admitted to the ICU when it flares up and she can't breathe."

"She's young and pulmonary hypertension is a good reason to be on the lung transplant list. Hopefully, she'll do better than most." Joe shook his head, then straightened his beard when it slipped. "Poor kids. I hope their mom gets a chance at a second life soon."

"Me, too." Dana didn't have time to say more as the next child was already climbing onto Joe's lap.

One of the kids stepped on her foot. "Ouch." She reached down to massage her toes through the felt elf shoes. "No fighting with the balloons," she warned, using her best stern voice as two boys set out to knock each other silly.

The boys stopped batting each other long enough to glance up at her, then went at it again. Feeling a headache begin to throb along her temple, she motioned for one of the other elves, Susan from Physical Therapy, to take over the job of keeping the kids in line and handing out the gift stockings. Then she inched over to where Jessica sat near her children.

"Santa is, too, magic." Wendy looked close to tears as she stared mutinously at her brother, tiny hands propped on her hips. Dana's heart went out to the little girl. "He can so get Mommy a new set of lungs."

"You're such a baby," Chad argued in a dismissive tone. "Stop talking about it. You're upsetting Mom."

Dana was willing to bet that it was listening to her kids arguing rather than anything Wendy had said that was causing the strain on Jessica's features. She stepped closer, ready to intervene. "Hi Jessica. Are these your children? I can't believe how much they've grown since I last saw them."

"Yes, they're…growing like weeds…every day." Jessica had to pause often to take a breath, but she appeared grateful for the interruption. "You're cute…as an elf…Dana."

"Guess my disguise isn't working real well, huh?" Dana flashed a rueful smile as she gave the tights another subtle hike. She turned towards Wendy and Chad. "Are you two hungry? There's cookies and punch over there." Dana gestured to the other side of the room, where a group of kids had gathered in front of a long table laden with treats.

"Cookies?" Chad's attention was successfully diverted to food. "Cool. Do you want one Mom?"

"No, thanks… You both…go ahead." Jessica watched them run off.

"How are you really feeling, Jessica?" Dana noted

the dusky tinge around the woman's mouth with concern. "Have you been seen in the clinic lately?"

"Yes. I was…just admitted…yesterday…to a room…on Four West." Jessica sighed. "I'm hoping…they can adjust…my meds…so I can go…home soon."

Jessica didn't look well enough to be discharged but before Dana could say anything more, there was a muffled cry from halfway across the room. She turned in time to see the two rowdy boys hit Wendy hard enough to knock her backwards, off her feet.

"Hey!" Dana rushed over to Wendy, giving the boys a stern look. "I already told you, no fighting."

She set the girl on her feet, and to her surprise Wendy wrapped her arms around Dana's legs and buried her face in the green fabric of her tunic.

"What's wrong, Wendy? Did those boys hurt you?" Dana gently stroked Wendy's hair.

"No." Wendy shook her head, then peered up at Dana through tear-tipped lashes. "Do you think Santa is magic?"

"Ah…sure I do." Was she wrong to encourage the child to believe in magic and miracles when she didn't believe in them herself? Maybe. Yet she couldn't bring herself to wipe the blatant hope from Wendy's bright eyes.

"Really?" Wendy's lower lip trembled. "Or are you just saying that because you're dressed like an elf?"

The mere mention of the annoying elf costume made her legs itch. She subtly rubbed one leg over the other, then bent down to smooth a hand over Wendy's bright silky red hair. "Sweetheart, I think there is all sorts of magic in the world. Love is just like magic. You love your mother and she loves you. There's nothing more powerful than that."

For a moment Wendy clung to her legs, then finally her expression cleared and she let go. Dana took her hand and walked her back to where her mother waited. Chad joined them soon afterwards and once the boy had stuffed the last bit of cookie in his mouth, he promptly took charge of his mom's wheelchair.

"Bye, Jessica. I'll come up to visit before I start my shift." Dana waved as Chad wheeled his mom away.

Dana watched them walk off, the kids acting very adult-like as they took care to make sure Jessica's wheelchair didn't hit anything. The knot in her belly grew as she suspected there wasn't enough magic in the world to ensure Jessica received a lung transplant as a Christmas present.

Poor Wendy. Dana couldn't stand the thought of the little girl being so upset and disappointed, especially during the holiday season.

Dana straightened her shoulders. Finding the holiday spirit would be difficult to do for her own sake, but she could support Jessica's kids. Maybe she couldn't give Jessica a new pair of lungs, but she could remain positive enough to help boost holiday morale for her patients and their families.

And in doing so, she'd fulfill the promise she'd made to her mother.

After making two wrong turns, Dr. Mitch Reynolds finally found the cafeteria, but the place looked like a war zone. Kids dashed from one side of the room to the other among a sea of red, green and white balloons. The familiar pang of longing pierced his heart and his appetite evaporated. He was turning away, intent on putting as much distance between himself and the painful reminder as he could, when he caught sight of a petite brunette, wearing a strange elf costume, hugging a child who'd wrapped her arms around her legs.

Arrested by the image, he froze. The woman wasn't classically beautiful, but pretty, in spite of the neon-green tights and tunic. What held his attention was the way she tended to the child, smoothing a hand over the girl's bright red hair and smiling down at her with a caring, compassionate gaze.

The perfect cameo of a mother. He closed his eyes for a moment, then, when he looked again, he realized the brunette elf was leading the girl towards a woman seated in a wheelchair. Soon a boy joined them and the two kids pushed the woman in the wheelchair towards the elevator, leaving the elf behind. The woman in the wheelchair and the two kids all shared the same bright red hair.

Apparently the cute elf wasn't the girl's mother.

He shook off the ridiculous thought. What difference did it make? Meeting women wasn't high on his list of priorities at the moment. He definitely wasn't in the market for another woman or a family. Bells jangled at the elf's wrists and ankles when she walked over to break up a fight between two boys who kept swatting at other kids with their balloons. His gaze lingered on her legs, until he pulled himself together.

Enough. The cute elf wasn't his concern. In fact, if he were smart he'd stay far away from any hint of temptation. Abandoning the cafeteria, he headed for the deli on the other side of the hospital. Someone had mentioned the deli wasn't fully operational on the weekends, but there were cold sandwiches available in the various vending machines. To his mind, vending-machine food was a far better option than facing the crowd of kids in the cafeteria.

Mitch sighed and jammed his hands into the pockets of his lab coat. The chief of pulmonary/critical care medicine, Dr. Ed Jericho, had recruited him to Trinity Medical Center from Kansas City University Hospital. So far, the change of scenery had been good for him. Milwaukee was surprisingly nice, a combination of big city and small town packed into one. If not for the holiday decorations haunting him at every turn, he'd feel better about his decision to move, to start over after two of the worst years of his life.

The bitter taste of anguish lingered on his tongue. Although he'd had two years to work his way through the maze of grief, the holidays were always the hardest to face. A constant reminder of everything he'd loved and lost. But the holiday theme would have been a problem no matter where he worked. At least the job here at Trinity Medical Center was a good one. He loved the challenge of critical care and with this position as an assistant professor he could take care of patients and teach new residents.

Starting over, creating a new life for himself.

He found the deli much quieter than the cafeteria. After feeding a couple of dollar bills into the slot of a vending machine, he took his sandwich and sat at one of the empty seats. The ham and swiss on rye tasted like rubber, but he wasn't all that hungry anyway. Glancing at his watch, he figured he had at least another ten minutes before he needed to get back up to the ICU. He'd finished making rounds, but still needed to write daily progress notes on all the patients under his care.

"Code Blue, Four West. Code Blue, Four West." The overhead announcement propelled him to his feet.

Four West? He tossed the remains of his ham on rye in the garbage on his way out the door. He had a vague idea where the Four-West wing was, and even though his residents would respond, he wanted to be there to supervise his first emergency situation here at Trinity.

Adrenaline kicked in as he ran up the stairs to the fourth floor. Breathless, he reached the landing, then followed the rest of the Code Blue responders as they dashed toward a patient's room, where a crash cart was being rolled inside.

"Wait! Don't intubate her yet." A female voice rose in agitation above the din. "She has pulmonary hypertension. Just bag her for a few minutes."

Mitch entered the room, and somehow wasn't shocked to find the brunette elf holding off the anesthesiologist, who appeared very annoyed.

"What's going on?"

The elf turned toward him. "Jessica Kinkade has pulmonary hypertension and is on the lung transplant list.

If you intubate her, you'll never be able to get the tube out. I really think we should try a non-invasive method to improve her oxygenation first."

"And who are you?" Mitch moved to the patient's bedside, recognizing the woman in the wheelchair from the cafeteria earlier. A quick glance around the room ascertained her two children weren't sitting there, watching the commotion.

"I'm Dana Whitney, one of the nurses in the ICU. I know Jessica. She's been admitted several times."

"Hold off on the intubation," Mitch directed the anesthesiologist. "Dana is right. We need to try a bi-pap mask first."

"I have one here." The respiratory therapist held up the device.

Mitch took it from his fingers. "Dana, has Jessica used this bi-pap mask before?"

"Yes." Dana's expression was tense as he removed the ambu bag and placed the bi-pap mask over the patient's nose and mouth. With the respiratory therapist's help, they connected the apparatus so that there was an additional push of pressure with every breath Jessica took.

"I'd like to give her a touch of Versed to relax her. These bi-pap masks are difficult to tolerate."

"I know." Dana frowned, trying to remember. "I believe we used Versed before with her, but in small amounts."

"Let's start with one milligram." Mitch kept his eye on the pulse oximeter reading, showing an oxygen saturation of 80 percent. Pretty low, even with PPH primary pulmonary hypertension. He'd rather see the number a little closer to ninety percent.

"Sounds good," Dana agreed, looking relieved.

He nodded to the medication administration nurse standing on the other side of the bed. At his signal, she bent to inject the Versed into Jessica's IV.

The rest of the Code Blue team stood back to let Dana and Mitch take care of the situation. For a moment their gazes collided, and he was startled when a flash of awareness sprang between them. He tore his gaze away with an effort. He couldn't deny he was glad elf Dana was here to help guide him, since he wasn't nearly as familiar with the patient's history as she was.

"Pulse ox is up to 88 percent," Dana announced with relief. "Much better."

"Yeah, but I'd still like to keep an eye on her in the ICU for at least twenty-four hours." He couldn't help raking his gaze over Dana's green attire, only partially covered by the paper gown she'd donned when Jessica's condition had deteriorated. As much as he appreciated a nice pair of legs, the green tights were a bit much. "Are you actually on duty in that get-up?"

She blushed and self-consciously tugged the paper gown over her tunic. "Not yet. I start at three. I was on my way to visit Jessica when the code was called."

"If you don't mind, maybe you could punch in early. I could use your help to get up to speed on Ms. Kinkade's medical history."

She stared for a minute at his name printed across the upper left breast pocket of his lab coat. They'd never met but he figured she'd recognize his name as the new attending on duty. "Certainly, Dr. Reynolds." For some reason her crisp response made him want to grin. "But first I need to let Chad and Wendy know what's going on."

The patient's children. His smile faded. "Of course." He turned to the resident who was supposed to be in charge of the Code Blue who but hadn't said a word while Dana had argued with the anesthesiologist. "Steve, I'm trusting you to get Ms. Kinkade safely transferred to the ICU. Once you get there, prepare to place an arterial line but wait for me before you start the procedure."

"Yes sir." The resident nodded.

"Do you have any questions?" Mitch had his doubts about the resident's ability to handle the simple transfer. The guy hadn't exactly stepped up to take a leadership role during the emergency situation.

"No, sir." The resident shook his head.

"Good. I'll meet you over there in a few minutes."

"I can talk to the kids myself," Dana protested.

"No." As much as he wanted to avoid the task, avoid the children, his sense of duty wouldn't let him. He rubbed a hand over his stomach as if to dislodge the heavy boulder of dread sitting there, forcing himself to stay when he really wanted nothing more than to follow the patient to the ICU. He gestured to the door. "We'll both talk to them."

CHAPTER TWO

DANA HAD HEARD about Dr. Mitch Reynolds through the unit gossip mill. Some of the nurses had already discovered Dr. Reynolds, the new critical care intensivist, was single but she hadn't really believed he was as handsome as they'd claimed.

She'd been wrong. With his dark chocolate-brown hair and square jaw, he was far more attractive than she'd ever imagined. One glance from his dark eyes had made her toes curl in the pointy-toed elf shoes.

The nurses had also mentioned that he'd been recruited from Nebraska. Or was it Kansas? She couldn't remember.

Either way, she wished she could have met him for the first time under different circumstances but, then again, there were lots of things she'd wished for that had never come true. No point in thinking about the attractive intensivist on a personal level—her luck with men was abysmal. Turning her back on him, she turned and headed into the hall, determined to help ease the news for Jessica's kids.

Wendy ran toward her, tears streaming from her eyes. "Is Momma going to be all right?"

"Yes, she's doing much better." Dana wrapped her arm around the girl, then glanced up at a very somber Chad. She included both of them in her explanation. "Her breathing is much easier now because we put a special mask on her face. The doctor wants to keep an eye on her in the ICU."

"No-o-o," Wendy wailed, then buried her face against Dana's thighs like she had earlier. "I don't want her to go to the ICU."

"Wendy, the doctor knows what's best for Mom," Chad said in a weary tone.

Mitch cleared his throat, drawing their attention. "I'm Dr. Mitch Reynolds. I'm the ICU specialist and I'll be taking good care of your mother while she's in the ICU."

In a very adult fashion, Chad stepped forward to shake his hand. "Thanks." Then he tugged at Wendy, trying to peel her away from Dana. "Let's go. We have to call Grandma to pick us up."

"Why don't you wait a few minutes before calling?" Dana suggested, giving Chad's shoulder a gentle squeeze. "As soon as your mom is settled in the ICU, you can come in and see how she's doing for yourselves."

Mitch frowned, but didn't say anything. Did he have a problem with the kids visiting their mother in the ICU? Surely not.

"All right." Ever the responsible one, Chad picked up the two stockings they'd gotten from the Christmas party then took his sister's hand. "Do we have to go down to the waiting room?" He was obviously more than familiar with the ICU routine from previous visits.

Dana hesitated. As a rule, children weren't supposed to be in the ICU family center without adult supervision. She didn't know why the kid's grandmother had dropped them off and left them at the hospital with Jessica—possibly to get in some last-minute Christmas shopping. The family center was one floor below the ICU, but if she were in their shoes, she'd want to wait someplace close by. "Why don't you come with me? There's a patient lounge right outside the ICU, where you can sit and wait for a few minutes. Then we'll call your grandmother to pick you up."

"Don't you think they should wait downstairs?" Mitch whispered under his breath as she led the way down the hall towards the lounge. "Maybe their grandmother should be with them before they go in to visit."

She glanced over the kids' heads at him in exasperation and slowed her pace. Keeping her voice low, she said, "I know the ICU is a scary place, but these kids are used to it. They'll be with their grandmother the rest of the weekend. For now, let them spend time with their mother. Besides, there's a huge Christmas tree in the lounge. A much better environment for them than the crowded waiting room."

"I'd better go help the resident with the procedure," Mitch muttered, averting his gaze and disappearing through the ICU automatic doors without so much as a backward glance.

Dana stared after him for a moment, puzzled by his strange behavior. Something was bothering the new critical care intensivist and despite the fact his problems weren't any of her business, she was curious to know what was going on behind those dark eyes of his.

In the staff locker room, Dana quickly changed into scrubs, then headed back out into the intensive care unit to begin her upcoming shift. Her name sprawled next to the charge nurse title for the evening shift on the grease board made her sigh. Good thing she'd come in a few minutes early. When she was in charge, she appreciated having a few minutes to review the patients herself before everyone else crowded in.

She was surprised to see Dr. Reynolds standing in the unit, apparently waiting for her as he stepped toward her when she walked in. There was no sign of his earlier reticence—in fact, he greeted her with a smile.

"Hi, Dana." His assessing gaze lingered over her proper attire, making her cheeks burn. She knew better than to think he cared one way or the other what she'd looked like beneath the baggy scrubs, but for some reason she couldn't seem to brush off his dark gaze.

"Welcome to Trinity Medical Center, Dr. Reynolds." She decided this was their chance to start over on a more professional note. She smiled. "Is this your first week on the ICU rotation?"

"Mitch." He took her arm and steered her away from the central nurses' station, where a couple of the day nurses were finishing up their charting, to a quiet corner off to the side.

When he let go of her arm, she could swear she still

felt the searing imprint of his fingers against her skin. Her blush deepened and she bemoaned her fair skin. "Uh, is something wrong?"

"Fill me in on Jessica Kinkade's past medical history, if you don't mind." His low voice was rich and smooth, like cream.

For a moment she almost told him to go and read the chart for himself, but bit back the uncharitable comment before it could spring free. It wasn't his fault she'd been assigned in charge. She rubbed a hand over her thigh because even though she'd taken off the green tights, her legs still itched. Thinking back, she tried to remember what she knew about Jessica's case.

"Jessica Kinkade was first diagnosed with pulmonary hypertension four years ago. I remember because Wendy was only three years old at the time. She wasn't diagnosed right away, not until after the disease had progressed pretty far. She didn't respond to calcium channel blockers, but was stable on intravenous Prostacyclin until last year, when she was switched to the new drug, Romadylin."

"Prior to showing symptoms of the disease, was she ever put on diet pills?" Mitch asked with a frown.

"Not that I'm aware of." All of her memories of Jessica were of a very thin woman but that had only been since she'd become ill.

"If she has primary pulmonary hypertension, she's a better candidate for a lung transplant." He must have sensed her confusion. "There was a patient back in Kansas who ended up with symptoms after months of taking diet pills. She wasn't my patient, but I covered her care for a week while her primary physician was on vacation."

"Oh, I see." She nodded, understanding his apparent interest. "Jessica was put on the transplant list once they started the Romadylin."

"Because patients can't be listed for a transplant until they fail Prostacyclin therapy," Mitch added thoughtfully. "What about her social situation? I know she has two kids, but what about the kid's father? Is he still in the picture?"

"Sort of." For a moment the fuzzy image of her own father, whom she hadn't seen since her childhood, filled her mind. She'd gotten over the pain of being abandoned long ago. Only on rare occasions, like now, did he pop into her head. Stupid to dwell on things she couldn't change. She tore her thoughts away from her personal life and concentrated on Jessica's care. "They split up shortly after she was diagnosed, and I've only met him once or twice. I don't know if he still sees the kids. And I don't think she ever formally filed for divorce. Her mother is her main support system, although she has a sister, too."

"Thanks for going through her medical history with me." Mitch turned away, then swung back. "You know, the way you stood up to the anesthesiologist at the Code Blue was very impressive. Your quick thinking probably saved her life."

"Ah…thanks." Her cheeks grew warm again and she knew this time Mitch noticed because a smile tugged at the corner of his mouth. That same intangible awareness sizzled again between them. Wary of the strange reaction, she caught her breath then pulled her gaze away with an effort. A small group of nurses was gathered in front of the patient assignment board, waiting for her. "I'd better get to work. I'm in charge and they're waiting for me to get a run-down on the patients in the unit."

"Do you mind if I listen in?" Mitch asked.

Heck, yeah, she minded. But, of course, she couldn't say that, so she lifted a negligent shoulder. "If you like."

She was keenly aware of Mitch standing behind her as she listened to the run-down on the patients in the ICU. She had been off for two days, but a few of the names were familiar. Especially Jessica Kinkade's.

"Thanks, Amy." She turned from the day charge nurse to glance back at the rest of her co-workers. "Let me know which patients you want to take care of."

A few of the nurses piped up right away, as they wanted the same patients they'd had the previous day. Dana didn't blame them at all, and accommodated their request. By the time the rest of the patients were assigned, she'd ended up with Jessica Kinkade as one of her patients. The other was a new admission from the previous night, a man with a subdural head bleed. He'd been reported as being a little on the agitated side, so she suspected he'd be a handful. As a rule, sedatives were never given to head-injury patients.

She started to listen to the day shift nurse's report on both of her patients, then remembered she'd left Wendy and Chad in the lounge outside the ICU. Glancing over, she realized Jessica's arterial line had been placed without any issues.

"Shoot. I have to get Jessica's kids. Give me a few minutes, will you?"

"Sure." Amy pulled a chart toward her. "Take your time. I have plenty of documentation to finish."

The kids were waiting patiently. Wendy had taken the coloring book out of the gift stocking and was coloring in the pictures. "Look, Dana." She held up her picture, beaming with pride. "Do you think Mommy will like this?"

The brightly colored picture was of a very elaborate Christmas angel. The picture was something her mother would have loved. Dana smiled. "It's beautiful, Wendy. I'm sure your mother will love it." She held out a hand. "Are you ready to go and see her?"

Wendy nodded.

In subdued silence, the kids walked along on either side of her as they entered the unit. Wendy clutched her hand like a lifeline. Mitch was at the bedside, listening to Jessica's lungs when they approached.

He didn't see them until he'd put his stethoscope away and stepped back. His spine stiffened and Dana would swear a curtain dropped over his dark eyes as he glanced at the kids. "She's doing fine." He gave a feeble attempt at a smile before turning away.

Wendy and Chad didn't seem to notice anything was wrong with him. Jessica was awake and when she saw her children, she reached a hand toward them.

"Mommy!" Wendy dropped Dana's hand to grab her

mother's. "Look, I made you a picture." Wendy held it up in her mother's line of vision.

"Wonderful." Jessica grasped her daughter's hand and looked at her son. "Love…you…both."

Talking with the bi-pap mask wasn't easy, Dana knew, so she stepped forward to explain to the kids. "Your mom needs this tight mask on her face to breathe, and talking will be hard for her. Don't worry, though, she can hear you just fine."

Mitch disappeared from the room and Dana wondered why his demeanor had changed so dramatically. She thought it was odd that he didn't try to communicate more with Wendy and Chad.

Did Mitch have an issue with kids? Both times around them he'd changed, as if emotionally withdrawing from the situation. Strange, because he seemed so nice. Maybe he simply didn't understand how to relate to them. He'd earned several brownie points in her book for insisting on telling the kids personally what had transpired after the Code Blue.

Dana didn't have time to ponder his odd reaction because as soon as she'd finished getting report, she called Jessica's mother to pick up Wendy and Chad then went over to examine her other patient, who was growing more rambunctious by the minute. She wished she could give him something to calm him down, but the neurosurgeons would never order any medication that might mask the patient's symptoms in case the head injury grew worse.

"Lyle. Mr. Tanner. You need this oxygen mask to help your breathing." She replaced the mask over his face for the third time in less than a minute. Even with his wrists lightly restrained, he managed to wiggle the mask off by thrashing his head from side to side and using his shoulder to displace the mask. She straightened it yet again. "Lyle, please, try to relax. You're in the hospital. Can you hear me? Wiggle your toes if you can hear me."

No response. She took a step back to look at the clipboard, hoping his neuro status hadn't taken a turn for the worse.

Without warning, he arched his back, then lashed out with his right leg in an amazing roundhouse kick. She reared back in the nick of time, the heel of his foot missing her face by less than an inch.

"Dana." Mitch was at her side in an instant, leaning over the patient and capturing Lyle's ankles firmly in his grasp. "Get some leg restraints."

She didn't need to be told twice, and fetched them from a drawer at the bedside. "Amy told me she had them handy, in case he got worse."

"Seems to me Amy should have put them on right away." Mitch's tone was sharp, and he scowled. "The guy almost kicked you in the face."

"I know. But the theory on restraints is to use the least amount possible. Amy wouldn't put them on unless she had a reason to suspect he'd get worse." She tied the restraint around one ankle, then threaded the end through a loop on the bed frame. "Hey, maybe he was only trying to wiggle his toes?"

Her attempt at humor was lost on him. His dark

brows pulled together in a frown. "I want these restraints on at all times."

"You'll need to write an order."

"Don't worry, I will."

Dana glanced back towards the nurses' station to where Lyle's chart was. "I'll get it for you."

"No need. I'll get it myself." Once she had the restraints secured, he moved away. "Be careful, will you? I don't think the hospital administration would appreciate losing a good nurse."

Wow, two compliments in one shift. When was the last time that had happened? She couldn't remember. "Thanks." She watched him head back to the nurses' station and caught the annoyed glance Therese, one of her peers, aimed in her direction. Therese's expression couldn't have been more clear. *Hands off, he's mine.* Dana raised an eyebrow. She hadn't arranged to get kicked as a way to snag Mitch's attention. When Mitch approached the nurses' station, Therese rushed forward with a fawning smile.

Oh, brother. Dana turned back toward her patient. As if she cared about the guy one way or the other, except, of course, maintaining a professional rapport with him.

Sweat trickled down her back as she fought to keep Lyle calm for the next few hours, in between making sure Jessica Kinkade's breathing and oxygen saturation levels remained stable. Keeping busy was good as far as making the shift go by faster, but she'd hoped for a little time to get some of the ICU's Christmas decorations out of the box hidden in the back storage area.

"Dana?" Mitch called her name from another patient's room.

"Yes?" She crossed over. "Something wrong?

"No, but there is a new admission down in the ED."

Bummer. She glanced around in dismay. Each of the nurses already had two patients. "What's the diagnosis?"

"Acute hyperglycemia." He read the message scrolling across his pager. "I need to run down to the ED to evaluate the situation. If anything changes, I'll let you know."

"Thanks." She wasn't used to any of the physicians communicating quite so thoroughly, but she wasn't going to argue either. A refreshing change, being treated as a member of the team.

"Are you making a play for him?"

Dana turned toward Therese, who had sidled up beside her. "What?"

"The way you're throwing yourself at Mitch Reynolds." Therese tossed her head, a movement that drew attention to her long wavy blonde hair pulled back in a bouncy ponytail. "You're being a bit obvious."

"You would know." Dana didn't have time for Therese's antics, especially when Therese had the most stable assignment in the unit. She tried to remain calm. "We're getting a patient from the ED—acute hyperglycemia. Can you take on a new assignment?"

Therese shook her head. "I'm already too busy. I can't handle a third."

Not too busy to come over and poke her nose in where it didn't belong, Dana thought, but bit her tongue to avoid an argument. Therese was the one nurse she had trouble getting along with, only because she seemed to care more about capturing a doctor husband rather than taking care of her patients. Therese seemed to see all single women as a threat to her personal goal. As if she could be a threat. What a joke. "Fine. Then I'll take the admit."

Therese flounced off, as if worried Dana would try to force her to take the patient anyway.

Dana crossed over to peek in on Jessica. Her interest in Mitch was purely professional, she assured herself. Her few relationships in the past had seemed to fizzle out, her boyfriends quickly losing interest in anything long term. She had no intention of going down that path again. Especially not with a guy as attractive as Mitch. He could have any woman in the hospital, and there was no reason to think he was interested in her.

Which was just fine, because a relationship would only complicate things.

CHAPTER THREE

WITH ONE GLANCE, Mitch knew the patient George Jones, his new admission, was in serious trouble. He turned to the resident on duty. "How long has he been vomiting?"

"Since coming in. He thought it was flu, but then realized something else might be going on."

"How long has he been a diabetic?" Mitch could detect the distinct fruity scent of ketones seeping from the guy's pores.

"Recently diagnosed, but probably had an underlying disease process for much longer than that." The ED resident was well versed on the patient's history.

"Do you have a set of blood gases?"

"Yes, Dr. Reynolds." The ED nurse, a cheerful middle-aged woman whose name he couldn't remember handed him the lab results. "He's acidotic, running a PH of 7.15. We started an insulin drip because his glucose was over 900. We've also hung mini-bags of potassium and magnesium to supplement his electrolytes. I don't like the looks of his EKG, though. I wonder if he has something else going on."

Mitch thought the same thing. "First we need to intubate him. Then I'd like to get him upstairs to the ICU."

"He's breathing fine," the resident argued.

"Not for long, with that level of acidosis. Intubate him." The resident shrugged, then headed over to do as ordered. Mitch turned toward the nurse. "I'm going to call upstairs to let the ICU know we're on our way."

"I need to give report, too, Dr. Reynolds," the ED nurse reminded him.

Already dialing, he nodded. He recognized Dana's voice when she answered and was annoyed when his heart gave a little jump. He cleared his throat. "Dana? We're intubating Mr. Jones right now, then we'll be up."

"Bring him up to bed ten, it's our only empty bed at the moment."

"Great. Here's the ED nurse to give you report on the patient." He handed the phone over.

Anxious, he glanced at the clock then back at the patient. The ED resident was taking his time on the intubation. Mitch shoved his hands in his lab coat pockets and watched, overseeing the procedure. He could have had the tube placed in half the time but unless it was an emergency, the residents needed to be in charge of doing procedures.

There wasn't a major rush to get the patient up to the ICU anyway, so why was he checking the clock every ten seconds?

Because he didn't have a good feeling about George Jones. He wondered if Dana would be the nurse assigned to the new patient. Then told himself he didn't care. He wasn't in the market for a woman. Especially not someone like Dana. If he dated at all, he'd choose someone who didn't want anything more than simple companionship. He wasn't ready for more. Dana was too open, too honest. She'd stolen his breath, the way she'd looked as she'd comforted Jessica Kinkade's daughter. Which meant Dana was off limits in a big way. He hadn't come all the way to Milwaukee to open himself up for more heartache.

He'd experienced enough heartache to last a lifetime.

"Dr. Reynolds? We're ready to go." The cheerful nurse drew his attention toward matters at hand.

Finally. "All right, let's move him."

Between the ED resident, the nurse and the respiratory therapist, they made their way up the elevator to the ICU. Dana met them at the bedside, jumping in to take over the patient's care.

Moments after the ED staff cleared the room, the monitor above George's bed beeped.

"He's throwing lots of PVCs." Dana frowned. "Do you want me to try a bolus of amiodarone?"

"Yes." He glanced down at the 12-lead EKG in his hand. There were some minor signs of a myocardial infarction, which might have been mistaken for a simple electrolyte imbalance. "You'd better get ready to cardiovert him, too."

Dana was already wheeling the crash cart over to the bedside. With a quick motion, she snapped off the plastic lock on the cart then opened the medication drawer.

He noticed she never hesitated, but with smooth, competent movements she gave the amiodarone, then hooked up the defibrillator just in case they needed it.

"What was his potassium?" Dana asked, staring up at the monitor with a frown. So far, the medication had had no effect on slowing George's heart rate.

"Only 2.5, but the ED has given him some potassium since that was drawn."

"The amiodarone may not work if his electrolytes are out of whack." Dana began to place the large, square defib patches on the patient's chest. "I'll ask Pharmacy to start a drip."

"I'll call for a cardiology consult." Mitch walked over to the closest phone, right outside the room. If George had suffered an acute MI, giving fluid, the normal treatment for DKA, might put too much stress on the heart and extend the infarct. After getting in touch with the cardiology attending, he hung up the phone and returned to George's room.

"He's in sustained V-tach but I still have a pulse." Dana's voice was calm. He was glad the patient still had a pulse because they had a better chance of converting him without sustaining too much damage to his heart.

"Cardiovert with 25 joules."

"We don't have bi-phasic defibs." Dana spoke up quickly.

Damn, he hadn't realized they still used old technology here. Without the new bi-phasic defibrillators, patients required a higher amount of energy, which could possibly cause more risk of heart damage. He'd have to have a word with his new boss. "OK, then, cardiovert with 50 joules," Mitch amended.

"All clear?" She waited for everyone to step back, then delivered the shock.

"Still in V-tach with a pulse." Dana glanced at him. "Do you want to repeat the same level?"

"Yes. Cardiovert again with 50 joules."

"All clear?" Dana pushed the button and delivered the second shock. For long seconds they stared at the monitor. "He's converted back to normal sinus rhythm."

"Good. Although I'm not sure how long his rhythm will hold." Mitch didn't want to take any chances. "Let's get the amiodarone going and keep replacing his electrolytes."

Dana nodded in understanding. Noreen, the pharmacist on duty, brought in the requested medications.

"Be careful with the fluids," Mitch warned as Dana filled another mini-bag. "Let's not stress his heart any more than we have to."

"I understand." Dana hung the medication then handed him the chart. "Write your own orders. I need to go and check on my other patients."

Mitch couldn't help grinning. Dana's blunt tone delegated him to the level of a green, first-year resident, but he couldn't take offense. Not when she'd been quick to recognize the defibrillator issue during the cardioversion.

When the cardiologist arrived at the bedside, he agreed with Mitch's assessment. "Once you get his electrolytes under control, we'll take him for a cardiac cath. I don't want him to arrest on the table."

Over the next hour they made enough headway with

George's labs that the cardiology team felt comfortable enough to take him down to the cath lab. He noticed Dana didn't relax once she'd transported the patient, but disappeared into Jessica's room.

"Of course I'll call your children," he overheard her say. "I'm sure they'd love to say goodnight. Just give me a few minutes to clean up my other patient, all right? I'll be back as soon as I can."

He understood Jessica's concern about her children. Parents never stopped worrying about their children. He shied away from the painful thought. The hour was late, well past the time he should have been heading home. Not that there was anything to hurry home to.

Although staying here to watch Dana run back and forth between patients would drive him nuts. She had more energy than anyone he'd ever known. And, technically, he owed her a favor. He stopped her outside Jessica's room. "Dana, is there something I can do to help?"

"No, thanks." Dana flashed him an absent smile then stopped, and came back. "Actually, there is. Will you call Jessica's kids? She wants to say goodnight."

"Ah…well, I don't know." He wished he'd just kept his mouth shut. Maybe he should go home after all. The residents could handle things here.

"I have the number." Dana must have been trained in the military by a drill sergeant, the way she thrust the clipboard holding Jessica's mother's phone number into his stomach. "Use the phone in her room, so she can talk to them."

She was gone before he could blink. Staring down at

the number, he wished he had just minded his own business.

Communicating with Wendy and Chad had been more difficult than he'd thought. He'd managed to avoid almost all contact with kids over these past two years. Not because he didn't like them, but because seeing them hurt. Watching Jessica interact with her children had brought long-buried feelings rising to the surface. The happy family atmosphere was a devastating reminder of what he'd lost.

For a moment he pictured with sudden clarity the moment of Jason's birth. The awe and absolute miracle of bringing a child into the world. For two glorious months they'd been a happy family. Then the day before Christmas his wife had walked into the nursery to find Jason wasn't breathing. She'd screamed for help and he'd run in to perform infant CPR, but to no avail.

The pediatrician had deemed the cause to be SIDS, sudden infant death syndrome. They'd done everything right according to the latest research. They hadn't put any blankets or stuffed animals in the crib with Jason, they'd put him to sleep on his back, they'd used a baby monitor. But still their precious son had died.

After that, things had gone from bad to worse. Instead of coming together after the tragedy, he and Gwen had been torn apart. He'd buried himself in his work. He had to admit he hadn't been completely surprised when she'd asked for a divorce.

In the space of a few short months, he'd lost everything.

Moving forward with his life had been the most difficult thing he'd ever had to do. Work kept him busy, maybe too busy. He still had a small box of Jason's things packed away. Maybe it was time to give them away, to the Salvation Army or someplace that would put the things to good use.

"Dr. Reynolds?"

He glanced up, giving the nurse who'd called his name a blank stare. "Yes?"

"Is there something you need?" The blonde nurse put a comforting hand on his arm. He resisted the urge to shake it off. The sensation was akin to that of nettles getting under your clothing, irritating your skin.

"I'm fine." He glanced down at the clipboard in his hands, remembering he still needed to make Jessica's phone call. He considered asking the blonde to do it for him, then realized he was being ridiculous. This wasn't a game of hot potato. He tightened his grip on the clipboard and searched his memory for the nurse's name. Her name-tag told him it was Therese. "But Dana could use a hand, getting caught up with her work." Then she could make her own darned phone call.

A flash of irritation crossed Therese's face. "Actually, I have a tiny problem with one of my own patients. Will you come and take a look at Mrs. Simmons in room one? She's running a fever and I think her lungs sound worse."

He glanced down at the phone number again. Not a priority in the big scheme of things, but then again his residents were supposed to be involved in problem-solving patient care. How else would they learn? "Where's Dr. Emory? Isn't she assigned to Mrs. Simmons?"

Therese's annoyance deepened. "I think I heard something about Dr. Emory being tied up with another patient. But if you're too busy, I'll wait for Dr. Emory to finish."

"No, I'm not too busy." He set the clipboard down, then headed over to Mrs. Simmons's bedside. She didn't feel hot, her temp was only one hundred point six. He listened to her lungs, thinking it was possible the patient had come down with hospital-acquired pneumonia. After a few minutes, though, he thought her lungs sounded about the same as they had earlier that morning during rounds. He took the stethoscope out of his ears and looked at Therese, taking a subtle step back when she hovered close, invading his personal space.

"Let's repeat a chest X-ray, just to be sure. Also, let's do a set of blood cultures and sputum cultures." He glanced back to where Dana was still busy wrestling with Mr. Tanner. "Have you made sure Mrs. Simmons is doing her coughing and deep-breathing exercises?"

"Of course." Affronted, Therese tossed her hair. "I just have a bad feeling about her."

Nurses' bad feelings weren't to be taken lightly. Mitch didn't say anything more as he scribbled the orders on the chart. "Call Dr. Emory when the chest x-ray is completed. I'd like to know what she thinks of it."

Turning away, he forgot about Therese. There was no sense in avoiding the task any longer. A simple phone call. Heaven knew over the years he'd called many family members at home and since he wasn't giving bad news, this shouldn't be any different just because he was calling children.

But it was.

He strode back out to the nurse's station, picked up the clipboard and marched into Jessica's room. She must have been waiting for him, because her eyes lit up when she saw him.

"Will you help me?" Her speech was garbled a bit through the bi-pap mask. "I want to talk to my kids."

"Of course." He took a deep breath, picked up the phone and dialed. When Chad answered, he was almost grateful since the kid was mature for his age. "Chad? This is Dr. Reynolds from Trinity Medical Center. Nothing is wrong," he said quickly, in case Chad panicked. "Your mom wants to talk to you."

"Just a minute. I'll get Wendy."

"No, wait—darn it." Chad had already handed the phone over.

"Hello?" Wendy's sweet voice made his stomach clench.

"Hi, Wendy. Your mother would like to talk to you." He held the phone up to Jessica's ear.

"Hi, honey," Jessica spoke slowly and loudly in an effort to be heard beyond the constraints of the bi-pap mask. "I wanted to say goodnight. Sweet dreams. Be good for Grandma. I love you."

"I love you, too, Mommy. Here's Chad." Mitch could hear the childish voice through the handset even though he held it up to the patient's ear.

Jessica went through the same ritual with Chad, then raised her eyes to his. "Thank you."

His throat ached with pent-up emotion, but he

nodded, then replaced the phone in the cradle. “You’re welcome.”

Jessica closed her eyes, as if the brief exchange had exhausted her. He felt just as emotionally spent. He turned to leave and found Dana standing there, giving him an odd look.

“Was that so difficult?” she asked, as if sensing his tension.

“Difficult enough.” He brushed past her, intent on taking a quick break. He needed to find the old familiar physician-patient distance he so desperately needed.

Downstairs, the cafeteria was empty. Most of the second shift staff had already eaten. All the signs of the children’s Christmas party had been cleaned away.

He sat at a table alone, staring down at his coffee. Jessica’s kids, Wendy and Chad, didn’t have a father. He was a father who’d lost his son. Gwen, his ex-wife, had remarried and was already expecting a child. He didn’t begrudge her finding happiness, although he couldn’t believe Gwen was willing to go through the risk of having another child.

Christmas tunes blared from the overhead speaker. He tried to ignore them.

No one ever promised life would be fair but knowing that fact didn’t make him feel any better.

Dana was the last to finish her work from her shift, and everyone else had already left by the time she punched out. Although her feet were killing her, she wasn’t quite ready to go home. And since things had quietened down in the unit, she decided now would be a good time to pull out the box of Christmas decorations.

She hummed "Jingle Bell" under her breath as she set up the small Christmas tree behind the unit clerk's desk. Hanging the small ornaments on the tree didn't take long and soon she headed into the staff lounge area to set up the second Christmas tree. This one was taller, so she had to stand on a chair to fix the branches along the top.

"Dana?" A deep voice called her name from the doorway.

"Yes?" Teetering on the chair, she turned. "Mitch! What on earth are you still doing here?"

He looked a little rough around the edges, his jaw shadowed and his eyes bloodshot as if he'd done an all-nighter. The hour was close to midnight and she'd thought he'd gone home long ago. "What are you doing?"

She raised a brow. "Hanging Christmas decorations. Would you like to help?"

There was a long silence, and she had to admit his lack of enthusiasm caught her off guard. Finally he said, "No, but I did want to thank you."

For what? She thought back over the shift. Nothing stood out, other than the few times she'd forgotten he was the intensivist and had ordered him around. For some reason, it was hard not to think of him as a resident. Maybe because he didn't carry the same level of arrogance as some of the other intensivists. "There's nothing to thank me for. I was only doing my job."

"I didn't realize your institution hadn't upgraded to bi-phasic defibs. I'm thankful you were there to tell me." He paused, then added, "Bi-phasic technology has been out for several years. There's no reason we shouldn't have up-to-date equipment."

"I agree." Dana placed another ornament on the tree. "The hospital went through some difficult financial times a few years ago when the technology came out. Things seem better now. I hope Administration listens to you."

"Anything else I need to know about?" Mitch asked, stepping closer.

The lounge seemed to shrink as he approached. From her perch on the chair she could look directly into his eyes. She was struck again by how alone he seemed, and for a moment he reminded her of Chad, Jessica's son.

She bent down, drew another ornament out of the box and hung it on the tree. "Not that I can think of. The nurses here are all pretty good, they'll help guide you if needed."

"Most of them are very good," he agreed. "Although I noticed you were one of the busiest."

Her heart warmed at his words, although she knew his observations were skewed. "Everyone has bad days now and then. Tomorrow it could be someone else's turn to run around like a chicken."

He didn't respond, but watched her work with an odd expression on his face. Much like the pained look she'd noticed after he helped Jessica make her phone call to her kids.

"May I ask you something?" She finished with the ornaments and jumped down from the chair.

He nodded, his expression wary.

"Why do you have a problem with kids being in the ICU?" Dana didn't tap dance around the issue. Better to know now if he had issues with her lenient visiting policies, because, if so, they were going to have a tough time working together.

"I don't. I just didn't think it was necessary to expose Jessica's kids to the level of illness we have in the unit." Mitch took a step back with his hands deep in the pockets of his lab coat, as if he was holding himself aloof from the conversation. From her.

"Those kids know the seriousness of their mother's illness," she pointed out. "Keeping them out of the ICU will only make them feel as if she's getting worse instead of better."

"Maybe." Mitch shifted his weight on his feet, clearly uncomfortable with the subject matter. "Then again, maybe not. Not seeing her at her worst may help protect them. It's a parent's job to protect their children from harm."

She didn't agree that allowing kids in the ICU was exposing them to harm, but the hour was late and she wasn't in the mood to argue. "I think you should know I'm a big supporter of lenient visiting policies. Especially when it comes to kids."

There was another long, awkward pause. "I see."

She was struck again by how he seemed to be pulling away from her. Now that she'd finished with the first box of decorations, she decided to save the rest for later. After shoving the empty box into the corner, she picked up her stethoscope and wrapped it around her neck.

"Goodnight, Dr. Reynolds." She offered a small smile, fully expecting he'd take his cue and leave.

"You called me Mitch earlier."

His comment surprised her. First he wanted professional distance, then he didn't. What did he really want? She wasn't sure if he even knew.

As if he'd read her mind, he added, "Please, call me Mitch. Dr. Reynolds sounds too formal."

"All right," she agreed slowly, sensing there was more to his request than calling him by his given name. "If you're sure."

"I am." His voice deepened and a strange, tingly warmth spread down her spine. In this moment, they could have been the only two people in the unit. In the entire hospital.

Are you making a play for him? Therese's accusation echoed in her mind. She gave a guilty start. She wasn't, was she?

"I'll see you tomorrow, Mitch."

"Goodnight, Dana."

She wasn't making a play for him, she told herself as he stepped aside so she could slip by. But when she glanced over her shoulder and caught him staring at the Christmas tree with a wounded expression on his face, she almost walked over to wrap him in her arms.

Ridiculous. Mitch's problems weren't any of her business. He was a physician with whom she needed to maintain a professional relationship, not a personal one.

She couldn't soothe his pain as easily as she could comfort little Wendy.

But she couldn't deny how much she wanted to.

CHAPTER FOUR

DANA HEARD THE phone ringing and reluctantly opened her eyes. With a stab of guilt she realized it was already close to noon. Of course, she hadn't fallen asleep until well after two in the morning, but, still, lounging in bed so late felt decadent.

She scrambled out of bed then lunged across the room to grab the phone. "Hello?"

"Dana!" Her friend Serena squealed in excitement. "Guess what? I'm pregnant!"

"You are? Oh, Serena, that's absolutely wonderful." Dana grinned, running a hand through her tangled hair. Her friends, Serena and Grant already had a beautiful daughter, Sophia, who had just turned a year old last month. Serena and Grant had managed to find happiness in spite of a broken engagement years earlier, during which time Serena had been pregnant but hadn't told Grant. She'd gone into severe depression when her son had been stillborn. As far as Dana was concerned, if any couple deserved to be happy, Serena and Grant did.

"I'm just a few weeks along, but I wanted you to be the first to know."

Dana was touched. "Thanks, Serena."

Her friend murmured something to someone in the background then came back on the line. "Grant says he'll expect Auntie Dana to help babysit sweet little Sophie when it's time for this child to be born."

"Of course!" Dana laughed. "You know I love spending time with Sophie. Now, make sure you take good care of yourself and the baby."

"You know I will. Bye, Dana."

Dana hung up the phone in a daze. The thought of Serena and Grant having another child caused a warm glow to settle around her heart. Serena was her best friend, as close as a sister.

If there was a tiny pang of regret for not having a family of her own, she tried not to dwell on it. Just because she hadn't found the love of her life, it didn't mean she begrudged Serena and Grant one ounce of happiness.

She had the passing thought that Mitch would get along great with Serena and Grant. Then she ruefully rolled her eyes. What was she doing, trying to make herself part of a couple? Mitch had issues of his own, such as a lingering sadness that convinced her he wasn't emotionally available. At least, not for anything more than friendship. Besides, her luck with relationships wasn't at all promising. Dana figured there must be something about her that didn't inspire everlasting love.

Maybe she was too much like her mother. Her father

had left her mother when she'd been four. Yet on a professional level, her mother had been the most self-confident woman Dana had ever known. Until she'd succumbed to breast cancer, which had spread through her lymph nodes to the rest of her body.

Dana wished she could share the news about Serena's baby with her mother now. Overwhelming sadness replaced the warm glow. Her mother had longed to be a grandmother, but unfortunately things hadn't worked out that way. Moments like this made the ache of losing her mother all the more difficult to bear.

Dana tried to tell herself her mother was still with her in spirit, but it was still difficult to shake off the sudden loneliness as she headed for the shower.

Jessica was still a patient in the ICU when Dana arrived at work later that afternoon. She wondered if Mitch would keep Jessica in the unit for another day or if she was scheduled to go out to a regular room soon.

Dana winced when she realized she was once again to be in charge. Sometimes Therese resented how often Dana was put in charge, but the other nurse didn't say a word as she took the role.

She quickly scanned the list as her friend Caryn came up to stand beside her. "I'd like to keep Jessica as a patient, if that's all right with you."

"I don't mind." Caryn reached into her bag and pulled out a Santa hat. "Here, I brought these for everyone to wear. I noticed some of the Christmas decorations are out, too—and it's about time."

"I started pulling them out last night." Dana didn't protest when Caryn plopped the red and white hat on her head, she was too busy looking at the various patients. "Wow, when did Mr. Tanner get intubated?"

"I don't know." Caryn handed hats out to several of the other nurses, too. Dana was surprised when Therese put one on, expecting the blonde nurse to turn her nose up at the goofy hat. "Do you want him back as well?"

"Sure. Which patients do you want?"

Once she'd divided up the patient load, she sat down to get the report from the day nurse. Amy had taken Mr. Tanner again and she filled Dana in on how his head injury had grown worse, and the neurosurgeons had intubated him to protect his airway.

"Dana? Line one for you." Caryn interrupted their report. "Family member of your patient in bed seven."

Jessica was the patient in bed seven so Dana nodded. "Anything else, Amy, before I take this call?" she asked.

"Nope, that's about it. I'll be here a few more minutes anyway, so if you have any questions, let me know."

"I will." Dana reached for the phone. "Hi, this is Dana. May I help you?"

"Dana, this is Rick Kinkade, Jessica's husband. I just found out she was admitted to the ICU. Is she all right?"

Jessica's husband? Dana glanced into the room, but Jessica appeared to be resting with her eyes closed. She groped for the proper response. "Uh, aren't you and Jessica divorced?"

"No, we're not." There was a slight pause, then he continued, "Please, at least tell me she's OK. I need to know she's not going to die. No matter what Jessica might have told you, I still care about her."

She was surprised by his concern, but a tiny voice in the back of her head wondered if that was just a way of manipulating the situation for information. If so, his acting skills were award-worthy. Truthfully, it didn't matter how he felt towards Jessica—giving out detailed information went against the hospital's privacy rules. Yet she couldn't brush off his underlying desperation either.

"How did you know she was here?" Dana stalled for time.

"Chad called me. I still see the kids occasionally on weekends."

"I can't say much," Dana cautioned. "I will tell you that she's stable and may be able to go out to a regular room soon."

"Thank God," he murmured in a heartfelt tone. "You have no idea how glad I am to hear that. I've been worried sick about her."

Strange how she'd never gotten that impression from Jessica. Not that Jessica had confided any details regarding the break-up of her marriage, but the kids hadn't mentioned their father the other day either. "Er, do you want me to tell her you called?"

There was a long moment of silence. "No. Jess won't be happy to know I've checked up on her," he finally admitted.

"Her mother is the spokesperson we give all updates and information to," Dana informed him helpfully.

He gave a harsh laugh. "Yeah, well, her mother doesn't exactly talk to me either, which is why I heard the news from Chad. Thanks for telling me this much. For a minute after speaking to the kids, I imagined the worst."

"I understand." Dana couldn't help feeling sorry for him. "Take care."

Long after she'd hung up, she debated talking about the incident to Jessica. For the first hour of her shift, Mr. Tanner kept her busy, then Jessica's monitor alarm went off, so Dana hurried into the room.

"Are you all right?" Anxiously, she raked her gaze over the patient. Thankfully, Jessica seemed fine. The monitor alarm had been nothing more than artifact picked up through the wires from Jessica's abrupt movements.

"I'm fine—stiff from lying here so long." Jessica wiggled around in the bed again, setting her monitor off. Dana hit the silence button. "Can I sit up for a while?"

"Of course." Dana pulled a chair close to the bed and covered it with a blanket before helping Jessica sit up at the side of the bed. "Just sit here for a minute, to make sure you don't get dizzy."

"I'd like to call my kids again, too," Jessica commented.

"Are they staying with their dad or with your mother?" Dana asked, hoping she didn't sound too nosey.

"My mother." Jessica's bi-pap mask had to be taken off for the transfer to the chair. Dana kept an eye on her breathing.

"So they don't see much of their dad?" She couldn't help asking as she helped Jessica stand. Holding a steady arm beneath Jessica's, she waited for her patient to take the few steps necessary to reach the chair.

"Only on weekends when he's not busy." Jessica sat in the chair and grimaced. "I hate feeling so weak."

"You'll build your strength up over time, I'm sure." Dana reconnected the bi-pap mask, adjusting it over Jessica's nose and mouth. "It's too bad your ex-husband doesn't want to see them more often. Since you're here in the hospital, it might be good for your kids to spend time with him."

Jessica frowned. "We're not divorced. I couldn't afford to go without any health insurance and he agreed to hold off for now. He likes spending time with the kids, but I don't want them to get too dependent on him. He's not much of a father figure."

Why not? Dana had to bite her tongue to keep from asking about something that wasn't any of her business. Was he abusive? Anything was possible, but he obviously cared enough to call and make sure Jessica was all right. Dana sat on the edge of the bed. "If you ever want to talk, Jessica, I'm here for you. I'm sure it can't be easy, going through this separation while battling your illness."

"Thanks, but I'd rather not think about my marriage right now." Jessica avoided her gaze and tucked the edge of the blanket around her legs.

"OK, I understand." Dana stood, then moved the call switch so it was within Jessica's reach. "If you change your mind, though, let me know. I'm a good listener."

Jessica closed her eyes for a brief moment as if

fighting some internal war. "I know," she whispered behind the mask.

Giving her hand a gentle squeeze, Dana changed the subject, forcing cheerfulness into her tone. "So, how would you like some Christmas decorations in here?"

"Sounds good." Jessica gestured to Dana's hat. "I like the hat, but not nearly as much as the elf suit."

"Yeah, but the hat's way more comfortable than the elf costume," Dana confided. She made several notations on Jessica's vital sign flow sheet, then headed toward the door. "I'll be back in a little while. Call if you need anything."

"I will." Jessica nodded.

Dana left the room and almost walked into Mitch. He lifted a brow when he spotted her hat.

"What is it with you and the holidays?" he asked.

She didn't want to blurt out her promise to her mother or admit how hard she was finding it to keep, so she simply shrugged. "I enjoy spreading Christmas spirit. We have a hat for you, if you'd like."

He shook his head with a grimace. "No, thanks."

Mitch hadn't wanted to help with the Christmas decorations last night either. Maybe he didn't celebrate Christmas. Or maybe he was trying to tell her, without being rude, that he liked her as a nurse but not on a personal level. Get a clue, she told herself, taking a step away to return to work. "All right."

"Dana, if you have a minute, I'd like to talk to you."

He sounded so serious, she grew concerned. "Is something wrong? We can go into the nurses' lounge."

He turned and led the way. Once they were alone, he frowned slightly. "I overheard your conversation with Jessica. I'm a little worried you're becoming too emotionally involved."

"I'm not," she protested, crossing her arms protectively over her chest. "I'm a nurse. We provide emotional support to our patients. Of course I care about Jessica."

"I know. I do, too, but if something happens..." His voice trailed off and his frown deepened. "I just think you have to face the truth. Jessica is very ill. She could easily die. I don't want you to end up hurt."

The idea bothered him, she realized. "I can't help getting involved with my patients," she explained carefully. "I'd like to think it makes me a better nurse."

He was silent for a moment. "Keeping a cool head in an emergency is what will make you a better nurse."

She narrowed her gaze. Was that a hint? He didn't think she kept cool in a crisis?

She was about to jump all over him when he continued, "I just think you should leave the subject of Jessica's marriage alone." He turned to stare at the tree. "Some things are broken to the point they can't be fixed."

Her righteous anger evaporated when she sensed he wasn't just talking about Jessica's situation, but his own also. The hint of grief in his eyes ripped her heart. There had been some rumor about him being divorced, but maybe something worse had happened. She put a hand on his arm. "You sound as if you're speaking from personal experience."

"Yeah. I guess you could say my marriage was one

of those things that couldn't be fixed." With that admission, Mitch shook off her hand, spun on his heel and stalked out of the nurses' lounge.

"Oh, boy," Dana muttered under her breath. Mitch's reaction suggested he was still hung up on his ex-wife.

She tried to imagine the sort of woman he'd loved enough to marry. What had happened to break them apart? Was he hoping for a reconciliation?

Attempting to hide an unexpected pang of disappointment, she returned to work. But the Christmas spirit she'd tried so hard to hold on to persisted in slipping away.

Mitch was annoyed with himself for telling Dana about his marriage. What had he been thinking? He'd come to Milwaukee to start over, not to remain haunted by his mistakes.

Mistakes that could never be made right.

Overhearing Dana talk to Jessica about her marriage had annoyed him. Even if someone had talked to him about his marriage to Gwen, he didn't think anything could have saved it. Some things just weren't meant to be.

Pushing away his regret for letting the truth slip out, he went over to the physicians' conference room to review the most recent chest X-ray on their newest patient. He compared the current film to the one taken during the patient's last clinic visit, making sure there weren't any detrimental changes, before he returned to the unit.

His gaze immediately zeroed on where Dana stood behind the nurses' station. Scary, how much he was drawn to her.

"I haven't seen you since the Thanksgiving food drive." One of the surgical residents evaluating a patient for potential surgical repair of a bleeding ulcer stopped alongside Dana. "I hope your toes are fully recovered."

"I'm fine. Don't worry about it." Her cheeks grew pink.

Unable to stop himself, Mitch sauntered over. "Sounds like an interesting story."

The resident, whose name-tag identified him as Ryan Avery, turned to him. "I dropped a twenty-five-pound donated frozen turkey on Dana's foot at the food drive."

"It wasn't that bad," Dana quickly interjected.

Mitch's eyes widened. "You're lucky you didn't break them."

"I'm fine." Dana looked as if she didn't want to have this conversation at all. "No broken toes."

"Dana's a great sport. Despite me being such a klutz." Ryan beamed at Dana.

"You're not a klutz. Our fingers were half-frozen from the cold." Dana smiled at Avery and Mitch's stomach clenched. He had to restrain himself from telling the resident to get lost.

One of the other nurses poked her head out of a nearby patient room. "Dana? Would you come help me for a minute?"

"Sure." She looked relieved at the interruption. "See you both later," she added over her shoulder as she hurried away.

Mitch wondered if there was a budding romance brewing between Dana and the surgical resident and the idea made him frown. Dana certainly deserved to be happy, but for some reason he didn't like the thought of Ryan and Dana together.

Dana's alarmed voice from across the room broke into his troubling thoughts. "Mitch? We need your help over here."

He rushed over. "What happened?"

"She doesn't look good. Her fever is over a hundred and four degrees." Dana's terse voice conveyed her level of concern.

The woman in question was Mrs. Hernandez, a cancer patient from the oncology floor. "She may be going into septic shock. Has she received her dose of chemotherapy today?"

"It's hanging right now." This time the other nurse, Caryn, answered. He quickly figured out Mrs. Hernandez was Caryn's patient, not Dana's. "She's been running a low-grade fever all along, but this spike came out of nowhere."

"Stop the chemo. Let's work her up." He glanced up at the monitor. "Set up for a pulmonary artery catheter placement. And tell the pharmacist I want to change the antibiotics to something stronger, like vancomycin."

Just then the woman began to seize. Mitch wanted to swear under his breath. "Give her five miligrams of Versed. Turn her ventilator up to 100 percent. Does she have a cooling mattress?"

"I'll get it." Dana shot out of the room in a flash.

He tried to remain calm. "Where is Dr. Biloxi, the resident in charge of this case?" He asked Caryn.

"I haven't seen him for a while, but I can page him."

"Never mind. We need to keep an eye on things here." The triple beeping of the alarm overhead drew his gaze to the monitor.

"We lost her pulse." Caryn had already climbed up on the edge of the bed to start giving chest compressions. The respiratory therapist was manually providing breaths with an ambu-bag.

Mitch stared at the monitor with a sick feeling in his gut. He knew Mrs. Hernandez had gone into a pulseless rhythm as a result of her sepsis. The massive infection would be difficult to treat. There wasn't too much more he could do to reverse the condition. Even if he could start the vancomycin, antibiotics didn't work quite that fast.

Dana rushed back into the room with the crash cart. "Do you want me to give epinephrine?"

"Yes." Protocol demanded they walk through the algorithm, but he suspected nothing would help unless they could reverse the sepsis. And considering she'd been on chemo, the chances of that were slim. Chemotherapy prevented the body's normal immune system from fighting the infection.

"Is she a candidate for Zigris?" Dana asked.

Zigris was the newest and most expensive medication for treating septic shock. But the side effects came with a steep price. With regret he shook his head. "The risk of bleeding is too high. She had surgery for a double mastectomy a few weeks ago."

The blood drained from Dana's face, leaving her deathly pale.

He wanted to ask what was wrong, but the crisis at

hand needed his attention. He proceeded to walk the team through the complete advanced cardiac life support protocol. Dr. Biloxi had shown up, but Mitch didn't bother including the resident in running the code. Finally, when nothing worked, he drew a halt to the proceedings. "Stop CPR," he told Caryn. "There isn't anything more we can do."

Dana spun away and ran from the room.

Mitch desperately wanted to follow, but first he needed to take care of things with Mrs. Hernandez. He filled out the death notice and then called the woman's son to give him the sad news. When he'd finished, he found Dana in the nurses' lounge.

"Dana?" She was sitting with her back to the door, her face buried in her hands. He went over and sat beside her. "Are you all right?"

"Leave me alone," she mumbled.

"I can't." Helplessly, he wanted to do something, anything, to ease her distress. He didn't know exactly what had set her off, but it looked as if something about Mrs. Hernandez's case had hit too close to home. Gently, he cupped her shaking shoulders in his hands and turned her to face him. "Come here."

Surprisingly she didn't resist. Her deep sobs tore at his heart and he held her until she finally cried herself out.

"I'm sorry." She sniffed loudly and he reached for the box of tissues, handing her some. She eased out of his embrace to wipe her face and blow her nose.

"You have nothing to apologize for." Mitch used his thumbs to wipe away the wetness of her tears. She was so beautiful, even with her eyes red and puffy. "Are you better now?"

"Yes." She nodded and gave him a watery smile. "I didn't mean to fall apart like that."

"What happened?" He couldn't help asking.

"My mother died of complications from breast cancer last year." Dana ducked her head and sniffled again. "I should be happy at least my mom died peacefully at home with me, like she wanted."

Mitch didn't know what to say. His heart ached for her. He knew only too well the heart-wrenching devastation of losing someone you loved. Unable to offer any words of comfort, he acted on pure impulse.

He lifted her chin with one hand, then bent to capture her mouth with his.

CHAPTER FIVE

DANA FELT THE warmth of Mitch's mouth, quickly followed by a thrilling pleasure dancing along her nerves. She clutched his lab coat to hang on to as dizziness swept over her. When she sensed he might pull back, she tightened her grip and tentatively opened her mouth to taste him.

He angled his head and deepened the kiss. The rasp of his tongue against hers caused a stab of need, reaching all the way to her soul. Dana was so lost in the sensation—his taste, his scent—that it took her a few minutes to figure out his hands were on her shoulders, gently easing her away.

What? She loosened her grip on his lab coat and he broke the kiss, moving backwards to put space between them. Confused, she blinked and drew in mouthfuls of air. She stared at him but his expression was carefully blank, devoid of emotion.

Mortified, she ducked her head, knowing her cheeks were flaming. She took several deep breaths, struggling for control. Had she imagined his response? Was she guilty of doing exactly what Therese had accused her of, throwing herself at Mitch? He'd kissed her first, hadn't he? Although maybe his intention had only been to offer comfort, unable to cope when faced with a woman in tears.

She was the one who'd turned his comforting embrace into something more.

"I'm sorry." She had no idea what she was apologizing for, but she felt it necessary to take the blame for the moment of out-of-control passion that had flared with that one simple kiss.

Before he could respond, footsteps sounded outside the door. "Dana?"

When Therese walked into the room, Dana jumped up from the sofa, nearly tripping over her own feet in her haste to get away from Mitch. Therese frowned and glanced between them. The awkwardness of the moment blared as loudly as a trumpet and Therese's gaze immediately narrowed with a suspicious glint as she swung back toward Dana. "You have a phone call, something about a possible transfer from the floor."

"Thanks for letting me know." Dana watched helplessly as Mitch backed away, too, shoving his hands deep into the pockets of his lab coat, a curtain of indifference shadowing his eyes. Anxious to get away, far away, she brushed past Therese to take the phone call.

As far as she was concerned, Therese was welcome to try her luck with him. Clearly Mitch Reynolds wasn't interested in getting involved.

And despite still feeling the tingling sensation of his mouth on hers, she would be foolish to believe otherwise, even for a second.

Dana managed to avoid Mitch over the next few days by taking patients that were stable and didn't need much in the way of medical intervention. Of course, she figured he was avoiding her too, the unit wasn't that large. Still, on the morning of her day off she couldn't help reliving the horrible moment when she'd realized he had been trying to extract himself from her fervent embrace.

She groaned and buried her face in the pillow. His complete and utter rejection was so embarrassing. If only she'd pulled away first, she wouldn't be feeling quite so stupid.

Needy. As if she hadn't been with a man for months.

Gosh, but the truth hurt.

When the phone rang, she crawled out of bed, praying the call wasn't from Trinity, asking her to work. The energy it took to avoid Mitch was too much for her to take on today.

"Hello?"

"Dana?"

She frowned, unable to recognize the deep male voice on the other end of the line. Mitch? Her heart stumbled, then raced with hope. "Yes?"

Silence hung for a long minute. "This is Brian Whitney. Your father."

What? Dana's knees gave out and she sank into a

nearby chair. Her father? After all these years? Pulling the receiver away from her ear, she stared at it in shock. Then reality hit. No, of course not. It couldn't be. This had to be some bad attempt at a prank.

"If this is your idea of a joke, it's not funny." Dana tried to hide the tremor in her tone.

"Dana, don't hang up. I know this is a shock, but could we get together and talk? Are you free for dinner?"

Dear God, this man really was her father.

"No." Dana's hand shook and she gripped the phone tighter to make it stop. "We don't have anything to talk about. Don't bother calling here again. Goodbye." She hung up, before she could change her mind.

Rioting emotions raced through her body. She was twenty-nine years old and hadn't seen her father since the age of four. Twenty-five years. A quarter of a century. Three hundred months. Nine thousand, one hundred and twenty-one days. Did he really think that after all this time they could get together and chat over dinner?

A hysterical laugh bubbled in her throat and she choked it back with an effort, clapping a hand over her mouth to keep herself in check. Apparently he had thought exactly that.

Ridiculous. What on earth would they talk about? Nothing. She ran her fingers through her hair, as if to pry distant memories away. Desperate to keep busy, Dana jumped to her feet. First a shower. Then cleaning, a task well overdue. When that chore was finished in record time, she wandered around the house, lightly touching the Christmas decorations that had once belonged to her mother.

For years she and her mother had spent Christmas alone. Without her father. Tears threatened once again and she wiped them angrily.

Enough. Just because her father had called her out of the clear blue, she wasn't going to fall apart. He'd been gone for so long, his absence was a non-issue. She and her mother had shared a wonderful life. She didn't regret a single moment. Dana pulled herself together and decided to get out of the house for a while.

Christmas shopping for the needy kids she sponsored every year was just the task to put her in a better frame of mind. And she might just pick up a gift for Wendy and Chad. No one could stay cranky when shopping for toys. Grabbing her purse and her winter coat, Dana headed outside, intent on going to the mall.

But as she drove, she couldn't help wondering what had caused her father to get in touch with her after twenty-five years.

And she resented her aching need to know.

A crush of people filled the bookstore. Mitch had wanted to get out of his empty condo but he'd avoided the mall with its overwhelming Christmas decorations, holiday cheer and cranky shoppers. He'd hoped the bookstore wouldn't carry so many reminders of Christmas but, listening to the holiday tunes echoing through the loudspeaker, he realized he'd been wrong.

OK, so he would pick up a few books and leave. No sweat. At least he'd have something else to do at home other than stare at his blank walls, feeling sorry for himself. Especially after the way he'd messed up the best shot at a social life he'd had in months.

Mitch gazed at the back cover of the most recent legal thriller, trying to lose himself in the story. After a few minutes, he realized he'd been staring at the words without comprehending a single one.

Dana. He couldn't even concentrate on his favorite pastime because his brain was stuck on a tiny brunette who had somehow managed to wiggle under his protective skin.

Closing his eyes, he relived the intense moment of their kiss, her sweet taste more addictive than any narcotic housed in the pharmacy. For one millisecond he'd wanted nothing more than to stretch out on the sofa with her, bringing her intimately closer.

Then nausea churned in his belly as he remembered the wounded expression in her eyes when he'd broken away. The problem wasn't with Dana, but with him. She'd gotten too close. Feelings he'd thought long dead had sprung back to life, making him want things he could never have. A relationship. A family.

He shook his head, thinking he should have tried to explain to Dana, but in truth, when the blonde nurse had come in to tell Dana about a phone call, he'd taken the easy way out.

Leaving Dana alone to assume the worst.

But over these past few days he'd wanted nothing more than to go back to Dana to apologize.

He needed to get out more, find something else to occupy his mind. Dana was a danger to his equilibrium. He was too attracted to her for his own good.

Something whacked him from behind, dragging him out of his daze. Mitch took a step forward, moving out of the way, glancing behind as he did to make sure he'd given enough room.

"Oh, excuse me." The dark-haired woman laden with shopping bags glanced up at him. Dana. For a moment he thought his mind had conjured up her image from his dreams but, no, the instant dismay crossing her features on recognizing him was all too real.

"Here, let me help you." He reached for one of the bags slipping from her grasp.

"I've got it," she insisted. He ignored her.

"Did a little damage at the stores, I see." The bag in his hand was heavy and he wondered who she was buying presents for. Did she have sisters or brothers? Nieces or nephews? The idea of being exposed to more children almost made him run the other way. Yet he couldn't deny he was curious to know everything about Dana.

"It's Christmas." She shrugged as if that said it all. She didn't smile or look him directly in the eye and he found himself wishing she would. She shifted a few bags from one hand to the other. "Here, I'm fine now. I'll take my bag and get out of your way."

"You're not in my way." She was, but he was forced to admit he liked her there. He tucked the legal thriller under his arm, then reached for another bag. "Here, give me a few of those, then you can get whatever you came for."

With reluctance, she allowed him to take a few more bags, then glanced over her shoulder at the rows of books. "I only stopped to pick up the latest Cavenaugh novel."

Mitch smiled. It was the same book he'd come to buy. "Me, too. Here, I'll grab a second one, then we can get in the checkout line together."

"I still need a few children's books." Dana moved toward the children's area and he found himself following. "I'll just meet you down at the checkout, though, if you don't want to wait."

"It's no problem." The Christmas theme was more noticeable here, especially since one of the store clerks was dressed up as the Grinch who stole Christmas. If Jason had lived, he'd be two now. How would he have reacted to the big green Grinch? The other kids seemed to love him.

He glanced at Dana. She pursed her lips as she deliberated between several large, colorful books. Her dark hair swung forward, brushing along the edge of her chin, and he had to stop himself from reaching over to tuck the strands behind her ear. Her casual outfit, snug jeans and a jade green and gold sweater that brought out the green in her eyes, made her seem all the more touchable. Huggable. Kissable.

Stop it. He pulled his mind back to reality. What was his problem anyway? He'd never indulged in daytime fantasies before. And after the way he'd treated her, he doubted she'd be interested in hearing about them.

Luckily, Dana didn't seem to notice his preoccupation as she chose several large books, tucking them in the crook of her arm before turning back to him.

"I'm ready."

He swallowed hard and forced cheerfulness into his tone. "Great. Let's go."

They made their way through the packed store to where the checkout lines began. As they stood there, he tried to think of a way to apologize.

Dana rested her bags on the floor with a sigh. "Don't tell me you're one of those people who finish their holiday shopping in June."

"No, I'm not that organized." He glanced away, unable to tell her the truth. That in the past two years he hadn't done any Christmas shopping at all. And that there was no reason for this year to be any different.

"Ah. You must be a wait-until-Christmas-Eve type, then." Dana picked up her bags and moved a few feet as the line surged forward. "I'm glad to say I've finally finished all of my shopping with this trip."

"Hmm," he murmured noncommittally. As they neared the checkout counter, he added, "Wait for me, and I'll walk you to your car."

"There's no need, I've imposed on you long enough."

He shook his head. Since bumping into Dana, he was loath to go back to his condo alone. "What if I told you how much I like spending time with you?"

She looked surprised as she turned toward him. "I guess I never considered how difficult it must be to move to a new area where you don't know anyone."

"I'm getting to know people here, but only a few I

care to spend time with." Mitch lifted his chin in the direction of the cashier's desk. "You're up, Dana."

"Oh." She picked up her bags and hurried over to the counter to pay for her books. Mitch still had her Cavenaugh novel in his hand and when another register opened up, he paid for both copies. Afterwards, he tucked the extra copy in one of the shopping bags he was carrying for her.

Then he caught up with her at the door. "I still have your shopping bags," he reminded her. "You'll have to direct me to where you parked."

"Sure." Dana led the way outside and conversation stalled as they bent into the bitter north wind. The snow from the previous night had melted into slush, then refrozen into ice. Twice he saw Dana slip before she caught herself and regained her footing.

"This is it." She popped the trunk of her white Mustang and he stored the bags he carried alongside hers. After slamming the trunk, she gestured to the car. "Get in."

He didn't argue, but slid into the passenger seat. She turned on the engine and waited for it to heat up. "Brr, it's cold. Thanks for helping with my bags. I'll drive you to where you left your car."

"How about we go out for dinner instead?" he suggested, glancing at his watch. "It's past seven."

For a moment he thought she was going to turn him down flat. Then she glanced at him. "Why?"

"Because I'm hungry?" She gave him a skeptical glance and he could have hit himself for the offhand remark. Reaching over, he took her hand in his, warming her chilled fingers by curling his around them. "Dana, please. Share dinner with me. I don't want to spend the evening alone and I like you."

"I'm not sure that's a good idea." Her words were quiet, barely above a whisper.

His stomach clenched with disappointment. "Why not?"

"Because I like you, too." The intense longing in her gaze nearly set him on fire.

"Ah, Dana." He reached up and cupped her cheek with his hand, then brushed his thumb over her porcelain skin. "I'm sorry," he murmured. "I don't have much to offer a woman right now except friendship."

"Friendship." She drew in a deep breath, then angled her chin away from his touch. "I guess you can't have too many friends."

He ground his teeth in frustration, wishing he could offer her more. Everything his body ached to offer. But it wouldn't be fair to Dana. He just couldn't risk falling in love again.

"Friends are important." He was lying through his teeth because he'd never wanted any of his friends the way he wanted her. "So, how about dinner?"

"No, I'm afraid not." Dana shook her head. "But thanks for asking. Maybe another time?"

She gave him an expectant look that told him she wanted him out of her car. Mitch wished he could stay, but took the hint and opened his door. He could walk to his car.

"Goodbye, Dana. See you at work tomorrow."

"Goodbye." The instant he closed the door, he heard the automatic locks kick on, as if she were afraid he'd jump in and force his presence upon her.

Standing in the cold wind, he watched with a sense of loss as she backed her car out of the parking space and drove away.

Damn. He wished he could be the guy she needed him to be.

CHAPTER SIX

DANA ENTERED THE hospital early, almost an hour before her scheduled shift. She'd wanted to drop off her Christmas gifts at Children's Memorial Hospital, then she planned to spend a few minutes visiting with Jessica, who had been transferred out of the ICU.

She'd tucked the legal thriller Mitch had bought her into her shoulder-bag, hoping for time to read during lunch. It had been nice of him to buy it for her. She wouldn't have guessed they shared the same taste in reading.

The Children's Memorial Hospital Volunteers had been thrilled with the gifts she'd purchased. Feeling in lighter spirits than she had on her day off, Dana headed over to the Four-West wing of Trinity Medical Center.

She walked down the hall towards room ten. Her footsteps slowed when an empty room loomed in her line of vision. The mess of discarded supplies on the floor looked the way a room did after a Code Blue had been called. Feeling sick, she spun around to head over to the ICU.

She prayed Jessica was all right, that her favorite

patient had just experienced a little trouble with her breathing again and nothing worse.

Coming round the corner, she found three people huddled in the waiting room outside the ICU doors. The familiar tear-streaked faces of Wendy and Chad tugged at her heart.

For a moment she suspected the worst. Had Jessica died before the staff had been able to get her stable and transferred to the ICU?

"Dana!" When Wendy saw her, she ran over. Dana caught the little girl close. "Mommy's in the ICU again."

Thank heavens. "I know, sweetie. I'm so sorry," Dana murmured in empathy. The emotional roller-coaster of chronic illness wasn't fun to ride. "I promise we'll take good care of her."

Lifting her gaze, she noticed a tall, thin man standing beside Chad, but the lanky build so much like Chad's she suspected at once he was the children's father. When he saw her, he stepped forward, holding out a hand. "Dana? I believe we spoke on the phone. I'm Rick Kinkade."

"Nice to meet you, Rick." Dana took his hand in hers. "I'm sorry we couldn't meet under better circumstances."

"Me, too." His expression clouded. "We're waiting for the doctor to come and talk to us."

Mitch walked through the double doors from the ICU before Rick had finished speaking. "Hello. I'm Dr. Reynolds, the critical care intensivist on duty."

Since Wendy continued to hold onto Dana, there was no way to avoid him. "Hi."

"Dana." Mitch's glance encompassed the rest of

Jessica's family. "Hi, Chad, Wendy. Your mother is doing fine. She's breathing better with that bi-pap mask on her face, the same one she had before."

"Is she going to need that at home?" Chad asked.

Good question. Dana glanced toward Mitch, wondering how he would respond. He didn't lie, but slowly nodded his head. "She might, if she doesn't get a lung transplant soon. Her lungs aren't doing very well on their own."

Chad hunched his shoulders and stared at his feet. Dana wondered if he was trying not to cry. She ached for the boy. What could she say? How do you prepare a child for the all-too-real possibility of losing his mother?

"Dana? Would you, please, show the kids to bed three?" Mitch asked. "I promised Jessica I'd send them in."

Assuming he wanted to talk to Jessica's husband alone, she nodded and turned toward Chad. "Uh, sure. Are you guys ready to go in?"

The boy hesitated and Dana was struck by the way he subtly stayed close to his dad. No matter what had transpired between Jessica and her husband, the boy seemed to need his father. And she was sure Wendy did, too.

"Go ahead, son. I'll wait here for you." Rick nudged Chad forward.

Dana led the way into the unit. As before, Chad and Wendy hung close to her side as she took them to see their mother.

"Chad. Wendy." Jessica's pale features appeared more fragile than ever before. It was just a few days before Christmas, the woman looked as if she'd never be well enough to go home. The kids crossed over to the side of the bed, within their mother's reach. "I love you both very much."

"We love you, too, Mommy." Wendy's lower lip trembled. "Can you breathe better now?"

Jessica's smile was mostly hidden behind her bi-pap mask. "Yes, I'm breathing fine. Is your father still here?"

"Yeah, he's out in the waiting room, talking to Dr. Reynolds," Chad informed her. "He's going to take us home."

Dana noticed that Jessica's smile faded. "Good. I'm glad. Just don't forget to do your homework."

"We won't." Chad blinked rapidly as if he was trying not to cry as he stepped back. "We'll call you later, Mom."

Dana moved forward. "I'll take the kids back out to the waiting room. Do you want me to bring your husband in?"

Jessica hesitated and Dana wondered if she'd pushed too far. But to her surprise, Jessica nodded. "Yes, please."

"Great." She waited as each child gave their mom a hug and a kiss, then walked with them back to the waiting room.

She found Rick sitting alone and wondered where Mitch had disappeared to. Rick jumped to his feet when he saw them approaching.

"Jessica wants to talk to you."

He perked up. "Really? You kids sit here and wait for me. I'll be right back."

As they walked into the unit, Rick halted her with a hand on her arm. "Wait. Are you sure Jess wanted to talk to me?"

"I'm sure. I asked her specifically if she wanted to see you."

"I'm worried." Rick dragged a hand down his face. "She wasn't expecting me to visit, then her breathing turned bad and they called a Code Blue. Maybe it's all my fault she's back in the ICU."

"Her lung disease isn't your fault," she reminded him. "I will grant you, stress isn't what she needs right now. But the last time this happened was almost a week ago and you weren't visiting then."

"No, I wasn't." Rick hung back, as if changing his mind about going in. "If I was less selfish, I'd do what was better for Jess and stay away."

Dana heard his words and abruptly wondered if her father had shared a similar sentiment. Had he thought he was doing her a favor by staying away all these years?

Impossible. Why would he feel that way? What could possibly be so bad?

"I gambled our life savings away, put us severely in debt," Rick confessed, making her realize she must have spoken her thoughts out loud.

"Not a good thing, but forgivable," Dana reassured him.

"Is she going to die?" Rick's expression turned grave.

Dana hesitated, trying to think of something to say. This was the most difficult part of her job. "It's possible. We're hoping for a lung transplant, but transplant patients don't always do well. All we can do is hope and pray."

"If anyone can beat the odds, Jess can." Rick squared his shoulders. "All right, let's go in."

She walked him to Jessica's bedside, then left them alone. As much as she wanted things to work out, Dana knew Mitch had been right. She had meddled enough for now.

"Dana?" Mitch came up behind her. "Are the kids doing all right?"

Whatever had been bothering him before seemed to have disappeared now. "As much as they can be, I guess."

He nodded. "I bet. This is the second time in less than two weeks."

"I know." For a moment it was simply comforting to stand beside Mitch, watching as Rick sat beside Jessica's bed and took his wife's hand in his. "You know," she murmured, "there may be hope for them yet."

She expected Mitch to walk away or disagree, but he didn't. Instead, he simply nodded. "Maybe. At least they're forming a united front for the children."

Knowing Mitch was divorced was one thing, but for the first time it occurred to her he might have children, too. Although she couldn't imagine he'd move away from his children. Unless his ex-wife had obtained sole custody. Highly unusual, but not impossible. Before she could stop herself, she blurted out, "Do you have children?"

"No. No children." His voice was low, raw as he avoided her gaze. His closed expression didn't invite further questioning either. Before she could think of some way to respond, Serena walked up.

"Dana, are you going to the staff Christmas party tomorrow evening?" Serena's gaze included Mitch.

"You're invited, too, Dr. Reynolds. There's a whole group of us going."

"Thanks, but I think I'm still on duty here in the ICU." Mitch took a step back. "I'll see you later, Dana."

"Bye." She watched him walk away. Serena poked her in the ribs. "So the rumor I'm hearing is true? You're going out with Mitch Reynolds?"

"No, I'm not going out with him." Dana watched him leave, knowing there was something Mitch wasn't telling her. Then she turned toward Serena and let out an exasperated sigh. "Who told you that? Therese?"

Serena had the grace to wince. "Yeah, it might have been Therese. Still, you two seemed rather chummy. You and Mitch I mean," she clarified, "not you and Therese."

Deep in the darkest corner of Dana's dreams, she wished the rumor were true. But she didn't confess that to Serena. Maybe later they'd have a chance to talk, when they weren't standing in the middle of the ICU. "We're friends. The poor guy moved here from another state and doesn't know anyone. He's just looking for people to hang out with, that's all."

"Hmm." Serena splayed her hand over her still flat belly.

"How's the baby?" Dana asked.

"Fine," Serena answered in an absent tone. "I'll keep working on Mitch to attend the Christmas party." Then she glanced at Dana. "You are coming, aren't you?"

"I'm planning on it." Dana nodded as they made their way to the nurses' station. As she took report on her patients, she couldn't help wondering if Serena would convince Mitch to show up at the party after all.

And if he did, would he come alone or bring a date?

Mitch put his hand in his lab coat pocket to pull out his stethoscope and a folded piece of paper fluttered to the floor. He leaned over and picked it up, then stuffed it back in his pocket. Not until after he'd fully examined the new admission did he open the paper to find an invitation to the critical care unit's holiday party.

He suspected Dana's friend, the nurse wearing the long braid was the one who'd slipped it in there. With a frown, he tucked it back inside his pocket. Attending the party would give him something to do, but he was wary of seeing Dana again. Or rather, he was wary of his physical reaction to seeing Dana again.

Sleep had eluded him in the nights since he'd run into her at the bookstore. He'd finished the legal thriller in record time, thanks to those sleepless nights, and wondered if Dana had begun to read her copy yet. Any excuse to talk to her again. He saw her seated at the central nurses' desk, reviewing a chart. When he approached, the unit clerk called out, "Dana? Call for you on line two."

"Thanks." His steps slowed when she picked up the phone. "This is Dana. May I help you?"

Mitch watched as the color drained from her cheeks. "I told you, there's nothing to talk about. I'm busy." She quickly hung up, but fumbled a bit as she set it back in the cradle.

"Dana?" Mitch couldn't help moving to her side. "Are you all right?"

"What?" She stared up at him with a frown. "Oh, no, it's nothing."

There was something about the vulnerable look in her eyes that made him want to hold her close. "Dana, there are laws against harassment."

"Don't be ridiculous. No one is harassing me." She stood up as if to get away from him.

"Wasn't that a call from an old boyfriend?" He followed her as she headed over towards Jessica's room.

"No." Abruptly she stopped and swung to face him. "If you must know, the caller was my father, a man I haven't seen for twenty-five years."

He hadn't expected that answer. "He's only just getting in touch with you now?" Mitch wondered at the timing. Had the holiday caused her father to call because this was Dana's first Christmas without her mother? "Maybe he's finally worked up the courage to get in touch with you."

Her eyes narrowed. "A little late, don't you think?"

While he understood her anger, he couldn't help feeling a little compassion for her father. "Maybe he's trying to make amends."

"Oh, please." Her smile was brittle. "Don't even try to stick up for him. Excuse me, I need to get some work done." She tried to brush past him, but he stopped her with a hand on her arm.

"I'm sorry, I didn't mean to interfere." Mitch spoke quietly. "But, Dana, trust me when I tell you life is too short to carry the burden of anger around with you forever. I know how detrimental it can be."

Startled, she stared at him for a moment, then her mouth thinned. "You're right. I don't like having anyone interfering in my life."

Regret washed over him as she wrenched from his grasp and hurried away.

The next evening, Mitch hesitated outside the Irish pub, his shoulders taut with trepidation. He hardly noticed the cold, damp wind swirling around him, bringing a light flurry of snow. Why he'd bothered to come to the ICU holiday party at all was beyond him. Dana had barely spoken to him for the rest of her shift last night. Why torture himself? Standing around, chatting and watching the various residents hovering around Dana, would be agonizing but at the same time he found he couldn't stay away.

As much as he ached over the loss of his son, Mitch found all those sayings about time healing wounds were somewhat true. Because despite having sworn off women, he couldn't ignore how badly he wanted to see Dana. To spend time with her. Taking a deep breath, he climbed the steps and walked in. His gaze found Dana immediately, picking her out in the middle of the crowd. She wore a tiny black dress that emphasized her curves and her eyes were bright with laughter at something Ryan, the surgical resident, was saying.

Mitch almost turned and walked back outside. What was he doing here? Hadn't he told himself over and over again that Dana deserved something more than he could offer? Ryan Avery was probably a much better match. What could he himself give her except a man haunted by memories? What did he hope to accomplish at a crowded party tonight?

At that moment, Dana turned and caught sight of him. Her face bloomed with a dazzling smile, but then the light in her eyes faded, as if she'd abruptly remembered they'd parted on less than friendly terms.

The brief flash of welcome in her eyes, though, was enough to make him weave his way through the crowd in her direction.

"Mitch!" Someone called his name, making him pause. Therese grasped his arm. "Hey, you don't have a drink yet."

When she tried to pour him a beer from a nearby pitcher, he shook his head, waving her off. "No, thanks. I'm on call tonight."

"Oh, too bad." Therese scrunched up her face in an exaggerated frown. He suspected she'd had a few drinks already. She spilled some of her beer down her front when she took a sip from her cup. "Whoops." She dabbed at her sweater, calling attention to her well-endowed breasts. With a coy smile, she leaned close. "We'll have to get together again when you're not on call."

"Sure," he responded vaguely, glancing over her shoulder to find Dana had managed to get a few steps away from him. "Excuse me, Therese. I need to talk to someone." He pushed his way through the crowd until he reached Dana.

"Hello." Mitch raised his voice over the din.

"Hi, Mitch. Merry Christmas." Dana lifted her nearly empty cup toward him in a silent salute.

"Are you still speaking to me?" He asked.

She shrugged, her grin rueful. "Of course. I shouldn't have overreacted yesterday. I'm glad you're here."

"Thanks for inviting me. Is that water?" He glanced at the clear liquid in her cup.

"Yes." She pursed her lips, staring into her glass. "I don't drink very often."

"I'm on call, so I was just going to order a Coke. Would you like something?" Mitch stepped behind her, toward the bar, and signaled the bartender.

"A Coke would be great." She downed the rest of her water and set the empty cup on the bar. Mitch was glad Dana wasn't the type to hold a grudge. Except, maybe, against her father.

The bartender handed over two Cokes, and he gave one to Dana.

"Thanks," she murmured.

"You're welcome." The crowd surged around them, bringing them closer. He put a hand on her back to help steady her. She stiffened against him and he tried to put her at ease. "You look beautiful tonight, Dana. I like the dress much better than the green tights."

She gave him a startled glance, then laughed. "Thank you. Although I'm hurt you didn't like my elf costume. 'Are you really on duty in that get-up?'" she mimicked.

"I liked your elf costume," he protested. No lie—the image of Dana in her elf costume, consoling Wendy, would stay with him for a long time. "Just not very professional for the hospital. But, I must admit, you have really nice legs."

Her cheeks bloomed with color. "Enough compliments already." She turned and waved a hand at the crowd. "Would you like me to introduce you to the others?"

"No." He leaned closer, breathing in the heady scent of her spicy perfume. If he could, he'd sweep her away and have her all to himself. "I'm happy talking to you."

"Me?" Her voice rose as if in disbelief. "I thought you were here to meet people. To make friends."

"Not tonight." Ignoring the sharp warning in the back of his mind that he was treading on dangerous ground, he leaned close to her ear. "I'd much rather take you someplace quiet where we can share a meal and talk. Would you mind if we left?"

She tipped her head up to look at him and it took every ounce of self-control not to cover her mouth with his. Maybe there was something wrong with him because the crowd was already getting on his nerves. He waited for Dana to decide. She looked a bit hesitant at first, then smiled and shook her head. "No. I don't mind leaving the party."

Her husky words sent his pulse skipping. "Good. Let's get out of here."

CHAPTER SEVEN

DANA THOUGHT SHE must have completely lost her mind to be following Mitch as he wove his way through the crowd, heading for the door. Serena, drinking orange juice because of the baby, gave her the thumb's-up sign when she caught sight of them leaving together. Dana flushed and misstepped, assailed by sudden doubt.

"Are you all right?" Ever solicitous, Mitch returned to her side, placing a supportive hand under her arm.

"Fine," she answered, even though she was anything but fine. What was she doing, voluntarily taking the yellow brick road to heartache? She'd been through break-ups before, but none of the guys she'd dated had really mattered much and more often than not they'd parted as friends.

What she felt for Mitch was different. There was a good chance he wouldn't just break her heart, he'd shatter it beyond recognition. She'd need a heart transplant by the time he walked away.

"Dana?" His earnest gaze found hers. "What is it?"

Someone bumped her from behind, pushing her

against him. Her brain short-circuited when his woodsy scent and strong arms surrounded her. He'd dressed casually in black slacks and a deep green shirt, looking far too attractive.

"Nothing. I'm fine." A tiny voice in her mind screamed at her to run away, to leave now and avoid getting hurt.

She ignored the voice of reason.

"We can stay here if you'd rather." Mitch must have sensed her uncertainty and his sensitivity to her feelings only made her want him more.

"No, I'm ready to leave." Maybe this time, taking a chance on a relationship would be different. Maybe this time, the spark that constantly sizzled and snapped between them was an indication that something more simmered beneath the surface of attraction. Something deeper. Heaven knew, she'd never experienced the sensation with anyone else.

"Do you have a coat?" He paused in the pub's doorway.

"In the coat check." She dug into her purse for the stub then handed it to him. "A long black wool."

"I'll get it for you. Wait here." He disappeared round the corner.

Dana shivered and rubbed her hands over her arms. There was a chilly draft from the doorway when someone walked in. Standing here, waiting for Mitch, seemed surreal, like she should pinch herself to make sure someone hadn't slipped her something to make her hallucinate. But no, he looked real enough when he returned, holding up her coat so she could slip it on.

"Leaving already, Mitch?" A brittle voice caused her to glance over her shoulder. Therese pouted and swayed, tipping the drink in her hand to a dangerous level. "We didn't even get a chance to talk."

"Yes, but I'm sure I'll see you at work soon." Mitch's smooth voice didn't betray a hint of disapproval, even though Therese was more than a little tipsy. "We'll talk then."

"Bye, Therese." Dana buttoned her coat, then walked through the door Mitch held open. As they left, Dana thought she heard Therese mutter something in a low tone.

"She's drunk," Mitch said dryly.

Dana chuckled. "Don't worry. I don't care what Therese thinks." Her laughter died in her throat, because she did care what the rest of her co-workers thought of her. And leaving with Mitch had sent a definitive message loud and clear.

Was it too late to change her mind?

"My car is over here." Mitch guided her with his hand. "Watch your step, the ground is icy."

When he opened the door of his car for her, she hesitated. "What about my car?"

"I'll drop you off here later." Mitch stood as if there was no rush. She slid into the passenger seat and tried not to jump when he closed the door behind her with a thud.

She rubbed her hands together, reminding herself that it was ridiculous to feel nervous. He'd only asked her to dinner, nothing more. Why was she letting her imagination run away with her?

"How do you feel about Italian? We could try

Giovani's. I've heard great things about their food." Mitch started the car and let it idle for a few minutes to warm up.

"Sounds good," she admitted. "I wasn't hungry until you mentioned Italian."

"Great. We'll give it a try." Mitch drove out of the parking lot and headed north. "The restaurant isn't too far from where I live."

"Did you buy a house when you moved here?" She was more curious about his previous marriage than she had a right to be.

"A condo." Mitch peered at the street signs, which were partially obliterated with snow. "I also live close to the bookstore, which could prove hazardous to my bank account."

She had to laugh. "I love books, too. Thanks for buying that legal thriller for me, by the way. I stayed up late last night after work, but haven't quite finished it yet."

"Do you like it so far?" Mitch expertly maneuvered the Blazer around a slippery curve. The four-wheel-drive made for a smooth ride.

"Don't ruin the ending!" She held up a hand in quick protest. "I can't wait to see how our hero gets out of the mess he's in."

"I won't." Mitch pulled up in the valet parking and handed over his keys to the attendant. Inside, the hostess took their coats before they were ushered to a quiet table in the corner.

"I'd love to start with a glass of wine." Mitch ruefully handed the wine list to her. "I'm on call, but if you'd like a glass, just say the word."

She shook her head. "No, thanks. I'll stick with water, too."

Mitch slanted her a grin and lifted his glass and touched it to hers. "Cheers."

He kept the conversation light and casual as they bantered with the waiter over the house specialties, then placed their order.

"Thanks for coming with me." Mitch's dark eyes captured hers from across the table. She had the absurd thought that she could easily drown in those eyes. "I hope us leaving together doesn't cause trouble for you."

Her throat went dry, so she took a sip of her water. She played nervously with her napkin. "I don't care about gossip. Although you know Therese will have us sleeping together by tomorrow."

"Really?" His deep voice made her shiver as he reached over the table to take her hand then rubbed his thumb along her knuckles. "Sounds intriguing."

She swallowed hard, realizing she never should have opened her mouth. If water had her babbling like this, she had no idea what damage a glass of wine would have done. "I'm sure Therese's version will be tawdry, rather than intriguing, so you'd better be prepared."

"My reputation has taken worse hits, but I'm worried about yours," Mitch said with a frown. "If she really starts something, I'll have to set her straight."

"Don't worry, I'm sure rumors won't carry to your ex-wife in Nebraska."

"Kansas," Mitch corrected. "My ex-wife isn't interested in rumors about me." At her skeptical look he added, "She's married again. And despite what you may think, I'm not pining away for her."

A thrill of hope warmed her heart. "You aren't?"

"No." He stared at their joined hands for a long moment then lifted his eyes to meet hers. The echo of pain in them made her catch her breath. "Dana, I really don't want to talk about my past relationship right now. And my ex-wife is honestly the last thing on my mind when I'm seated across from a beautiful woman like you. I'm more interested in hearing about you."

"There isn't much to tell." Dana didn't want to discuss the subject of her father with Mitch any more than he wanted to talk about his marriage, especially when they didn't agree. She wished the waiter would hurry and bring their food. "I grew up in Chicago, actually, but then my mother and I moved up here when she landed a better job."

"How old were you?" Mitch asked.

"About ten, I think. Anyway, we bought a tiny house in Wauwatosa, which was perfect for the two of us." She tried to shake off the wave of sorrow that memories of her mother brought on. "My mother was the strongest woman I've ever known. She was very busy at work, but always made time for me. She was an amazing person."

"Sounds like she also raised an amazing daughter. You must miss her very much." Mitch reluctantly released her hand when the waiter arrived with their dinner.

"Yes, I do." Dana tried to shake off her sorrow, focusing instead on her food. She inhaled the scent of shrimp scampi with appreciation. "Mmm. Looks great."

The conversation became less personal as they ate, sharing bites of their respective meals. Dana felt giddy and light-headed, without ingesting a drop of wine. Mitch had a knack for making her feel like the most desirable woman on the planet. Never once did his eyes stray to other women passing by. It was as if he only had eyes for her.

When their meal ended, she actually considered inviting him back to her place, then pushed the idea aside. Better that she take this newly found friendship at a slower pace. Besides, he'd only promised friendship, nothing more. Certainly not anything resembling a sexual relationship.

Too bad, because she was more than a little tempted by the idea. She hadn't been intimate with a man in what felt like forever.

Mitch drove her back to the Irish pub where she'd left her car. But when she moved to open her passenger door he stopped her with a hand on her arm.

"Give me your keys. I'll go and warm it up for you."

"Thanks." Dana handed over her keys, then waited, enjoying the rare sense of being pampered and spoiled as he started her car, then rejoined her.

"Give it a few minutes to warm up." Mitch glanced at her but she couldn't really read his expression in the dim light. "I had a really nice time tonight."

"Me, too." Dana couldn't regret her decision to go out with him. She'd enjoyed every minute. "And thanks for being so sweet, warming up my car."

"I hope we can get together again soon." He grinned hopefully. "Next time you can pick the restaurant."

Next time? Did she really want there to be a next time? And what about being friends?

Confused by his apparent about-face, she wondered what to do about the intense wave of chemistry shimmering between them. "I'd better go," Dana murmured. "I'm sure my car has warmed up by now."

Mitch nodded, then surprised her by climbing out of his car to meet her. Before she could open her door, he opened it for her.

"Are you working tomorrow?" He asked.

"Yes." Dana tipped her head to look up at him. "Thanks again for dinner."

"Goodnight." He leaned down to kiss her.

She expected a nice friendly kiss, but the instant his mouth met hers, the kiss morphed into something wanton, needy. His tongue swept hers and her knees nearly buckled. Fueled by a stab of desire, she pressed against him, reveling in the way his tongue explored hers.

A moan escaped, low in her throat. Mitch kissed her with an intensity that sent adrenaline spiking through her veins. Snowflakes melted against her face but she barely noticed the flickering coolness on her heated skin.

A group of laughing party-goers stumbled out of the pub doorway, singing "Frosty the Snowman" in loud, screeching voices. Reality intruded and she pulled back from his kiss, drawing in deep breaths to clear her head.

Mitch pressed a kiss against her temple, holding her close as if reluctant to let her go. Finally he loosened his grip and took a step back. His voice was low, rough.

"I didn't mean that to get so out of control. See you tomorrow, Dana."

She couldn't answer, so she simply nodded. He stood holding onto her door and waiting until she'd climbed into her nicely warm car, and gently closed the door behind her.

With shaking hands she fastened her seat belt, then put the car in gear and pulled out of the parking lot.

In her rear-view mirror, she saw Mitch still standing in the cold, hands tucked in his pockets, gazing after her with a serious expression on his face, while a light dusting of snow covered his dark hair. She wondered what he was thinking.

Was he also wishing the evening didn't have to end?

It took every ounce of will-power she possessed not to turn around and go back to him.

The next morning, Dana dragged herself out of bed and stumbled to the kitchen. Coffee. She desperately needed coffee. Double-strength coffee. If she could, she'd ingest only the caffeine.

Thoughts of Mitch had kept her awake long into the early morning hours. She regretted how she'd played it safe and left him, yet at the same time she knew she was already in too deep.

She was more than a little emotionally involved with a man who claimed to have nothing to offer her but friendship but kissed her as if she were the last woman on earth.

So she'd spent another hour trying to analyze her previous relationships, as if she might determine where she'd failed in order to avoid doing the same thing with Mitch. Until she'd realized that, in and of itself, was the problem.

While she might have some control over her own feelings, she couldn't control how Mitch or any other man felt about her. And it all came back to one thing.

No one had ever claimed to love her. Not to the point of not being able to live without her.

Trying to decipher what flaw she possessed had kept her tossing and turning for most of the night. Until she'd given up trying and decided to hit the shower then get ready for work.

Dana was in the middle of creating an omelet with the various leftovers in her fridge when her front doorbell rang.

Mitch? She couldn't prevent the leap of her pulse at the possibility. Wiping her hands on a towel, she hurried to the door.

A strange man stood on her porch. Irritated by being interrupted by some salesman, she opened the door and almost told him to go away. At the last moment, she hesitated, sensing something vaguely familiar about him. Was he a former patient?

"Dana?" The man, who she guessed was in his late fifties by the liberal sprinkling of gray in his hair, held up a white envelope with her name on it.

"Yes?" She frowned and shivered in the cold. How on earth had a former patient figured out where she lived?

"If you'd take a few minutes to read this letter, I'd appreciate it."

As she reached for the letter, recognition dawned. This guy wasn't a patient. He was her father. The man standing on her doorstep was the father she hadn't seen in twenty-five years.

"I know what you're thinking," he said quickly, sensing her immediate withdrawal.

"No, you don't."

"Please, give me a chance. I know you don't want to talk to me, but read the letter. Please, Dana, that's all I ask. Ten minutes of your time to read my letter."

He spun around and strode to his car, parked on the street in front of her house. While she stared at the envelope glued to her fingertips, he slid behind the wheel and drove away.

CHAPTER EIGHT

MITCH GLANCED AT the clock, feeling as if the day was dragging on forever. In reality things were busy enough, but he knew the real problem was that he was waiting for three o'clock when Dana would start her shift.

His pager vibrated at his waist, and he frowned when he noticed the message was from his Dr. Edward Jericho's office. Since Dr. Biloxi, the resident on duty, seemed to be doing a good job of examining the pneumonia patient lying on the gurney in the ED, he crossed over to the nearest phone.

"This is Mitch Reynolds, answering a page."

"Just a moment. Dr. Jericho wants to speak with you." Marge, the administrative assistant, put him on hold. Christmas tunes filled his ear but he couldn't dredge up the familiar annoyance at the irritating cheerfulness.

"Mitch. Thanks for answering my page. I need you to cover the ICU for the next two weeks, through to the first of the year. Dr. Ignasia's wife delivered early, and he won't be able to be on duty as planned."

Mitch didn't hesitate, although he felt a little pang of

regret at the news. A baby's life was so fragile. Too fragile. "I can cover, no problem. Hope the baby is OK."

"His daughter is a good size, at least four pounds, but they still have her in the neonatal ICU over at Children's Memorial. Thanks for being flexible, Mitch. I appreciate your help."

"I really don't mind." And he didn't, mostly because this would give him plenty of time to see Dana at work. Although he wanted to see her away from the critical care unit, too. The kiss they'd shared had left him wanting more. Much more.

For the first time in a long time, he felt truly alive, eager to face the day, ready to handle anything that came his way.

"Great. Any concerns, give me a call," Ed Jericho said.

"Actually, I did want to talk to you about the lack of bi-phasic defibrillators in the department," Mitch said quickly. "We don't have to get into it now, but when you have time I'd like to discuss bringing some in."

"Bring it up at our next faculty meeting," Ed instructed.

"I will." Mitch hung up then turned back to his resident and the pneumonia patient. Dr. Biloxi had finished his exam so Mitch wandered over. "Dr. Biloxi, what do you think? Does Mrs. Hammer's condition warrant an ICU bed or is she stable enough to be placed out on the general floor?"

He already knew what his decision would be, and he was satisfied when, after listing all the pertinent findings of his exam, Dr. Biloxi stated he felt Mrs. Hammer would do fine on the general floor.

"I concur. Write up your notes, then call the ward team and let them know they have a new admission."

At a quarter to three he headed back upstairs to the critical care unit. Dana was in the unit early as was her usual habit. He longed to approach her, but was mindful of the fact that she was on duty. Bad enough they'd left the party together last evening—seeking her out the minute she reported for work would only add fuel to the fire.

Not that cared for himself, but he was cognizant of the working relationship she needed to maintain with her peers. Especially women like Therese. He hoped Therese wasn't working tonight, too.

His pager went off again, this time announcing another possible new admission. Glad for a legitimate reason to talk to Dana in her role as charge nurse, he headed toward her.

"Hi, Dana. Thought I should let you know, there's a new admission on the way in, a sixteen-year-old girl who overdosed on over-the-counter medications."

She winced a little at the news but nodded. "'Tis the season, huh? Not everyone is cheered by the holidays. All right, thanks for letting me know. Since everyone else isn't here yet, I'll take Jessica and the new admission."

"Great." He gave her a quick smile. "I'm heading back down to the ED. I'll let you know one way or the other."

"I hope she didn't take too much," Dana agreed. She didn't quite meet his gaze and the furrows in her brow gave him the impression something was troubling her. There wasn't time to ask, though, because his presence was needed in the ED.

As he took the stairs down to ground level two at a time, he wondered what had caused such a difference in Dana since last night. He didn't like seeing her so troubled and wondered if she'd meet him later in the cafeteria so they could talk.

After years of keeping his feelings bottled up inside, it was strange how tuned in to Dana's emotions he was.

The ED was a whirlwind of activity. Mitch saw the hysterical parents first, then the group of medical personnel surrounding the patient.

"What did she take?" He asked as the ED doctor struggled to insert a nasogastric tube. The girl's name was Trina Grafton and she was extremely lethargic.

"Ibuprofen, aspirin, and some kind of cold medicine," the resident informed him. "She pretty much stayed with whatever happened to be in the medicine cabinet. Except acetaminophen, thank God."

Acetominophen caused severe damage to the liver, so at least Trina was lucky to escape the possibility of being listed for a transplant. "Let's get that tube into her as quickly as possible. We should intubate her, too, to protect her airway." The treatment for a drug overdose wasn't pretty—the activated charcoal bound the medication and prevented the body from absorbing it, but the only way to get the tarry substance into Trina's stomach was to put it through the tube. And pray she didn't bring it back up.

The ED doctor turned Trina's care over to Mitch as soon as he could. Mitch agreed to take the patient up to the ICU, but asked the ED doctor, Kane Anderson, to talk to the patient's parents first. "I'll follow up with them after we see what her levels are once we've given her the first dose of charcoal."

"Fine. I'll send them over to the family center once I've given them an update." Kane glanced at the young girl. "She's a cutie. What could possibly be so bad at sixteen?"

"How about a positive pregnancy test?" Erica, one of the ED nurses walked up to them with a lab slip in her hand. They routinely did pregnancy tests on all females of child-bearing age, just for this reason. They didn't want to provide treatment, especially medications, without knowing if the patient might be pregnant.

"Oh, boy." His stomach clenched at the news. He hadn't noticed any sign of pregnancy, although he hadn't looked for any either. "Get me a Doppler." Mitch pulled back the sheets and performed a brief abdominal exam, feeling only the slightest swelling in Trina's lower abdomen. When the nurse brought the Doppler, he listened all around her belly for any sign of the baby's heartbeat. Nothing. He couldn't hear a single thing.

"Either she's too early in her first trimester for the fetus to have a heart rate, or she's already lost the baby." He set the Doppler aside, feeling helpless.

"I'll get in touch the OB/GYN team to come and take a look at her." The nurse disappeared to make the call. "If the baby is still viable, they may want a continuous Doppler on."

"Are you going to tell her parents?" he asked Kane.

"Ah, hell. I hate this." Kane scrubbed his hands over his face. "Legally, she's a minor and the parents have a right to know her medical condition. But if the overdose caused her to lose the baby, it's a moot point. Should we hold off and wait to see what the OB/GYN team thinks?"

"I wouldn't." Mitch shook his head. "Her parents have a right to look at her chart. If they see the OB/GYN consultants in the room, they'll find out the hard way." Mitch silently agreed with Kane that this situation was the absolute worst. "Heck, for all we know, there's more bothering this girl other than just being pregnant. Either way, legally I think we have to tell them. No matter how much we don't want to."

Kane sighed heavily. "Since when are you the legal expert around here?" When Mitch raised a brow, Kane shrugged. "All right, I'll let them know. God, I hope I'm never a parent."

Being a parent was a huge responsibility. Especially when you failed to protect your child from harm. Losing Jason had left a huge hole in his heart. A rift so wide, he and Gwen had been unable to overcome the distance. After the divorce, he'd decided not to risk having another family.

Now he wasn't so sure. Was the pain and agony worth the effort? Trina's case was an example of how the risk of losing a loved one didn't only exist in those first precious months but throughout the child's lifetime. Thinking back, even knowing what he knew now, he wouldn't trade those few months he had with Jason for anything in the world.

A dilemma, no matter which way you looked at it.

He ignored the sick feeling in his stomach and called Dana to warn her they were on their way with the patient.

"Bring her to bed twelve," Dana told him. "I'll meet you there when I'm finished with Jessica."

Within a few minutes he and the ED transporter had brought the gurney up to bed twelve. True to her word, Dana met them in the room shortly thereafter.

"I want her on full ventilatory support," Mitch told her. "And get more charcoal ready—the dose they gave down in the ED came back up."

"I noticed," Dana commented with a frown. "Poor thing is a mess."

"More charcoal first, then we can worry about cleaning her up. Her parents are probably already in the family center downstairs, waiting to see her."

"All right. Give me a few minutes here." Dana made sure the respiratory therapist connected Trina to the ventilator, then proceeded to give the second dose of charcoal.

"The OB/GYN team should show up soon. Trina is pregnant but I couldn't detect any fetal heart tones with the Doppler in the ED. Maybe they'll have better equipment." Mitch gave Dana a quick run-down while she worked on cleaning up the mess from the previous dose. "We don't know how far along she is."

"Oh, no," Dana murmured, her gaze stricken. "What if something happened to the baby?"

"Kane Anderson is telling her parents the news now." Mitch sighed. This was why he didn't like the holidays. Nothing cheerful about this situation at all.

"Looks like this dose of charcoal might stay down. When do you want me to send more blood to check another aspirin and ibuprofen level?" Dana asked.

"Not for another four hours." Mitch leaned over to peer at Trina's pupils, verifying her neuro status hadn't changed for the worse. "I hope she wakes up soon."

"Me, too."

"Dana?" Caryn poked her head into the room. "Your patient's parents want to see her."

"All right." Dana continued to wipe Trina's face with the towel. She glanced at Caryn over her shoulder. "Go ahead and send them in."

Mitch stayed at the bedside in case Trina's parents had additional questions.

"Oh, Trina. No matter what happens, we love you. We will always love you." Trina's mother sobbed as she clung to her daughter's hand.

Trina's father turned to Mitch. "I don't know if you realize Trina is adopted. We don't really know any details about her medical history or any genetic problems she may pass on to the baby."

"It's all right," Mitch assured him. "Other than the obvious overdose, Trina appears healthy enough. We've asked the specialists to come by and examine her."

Dana stepped forward and introduced herself as Trina's nurse, then proceeded to explain some of the medical equipment in the room, including the ventilator.

"Why didn't she just come and talk to us? Doesn't she know how much we love her?" Trina's mother lifted her red-rimmed eyes to Mitch's. "Will she recover from this?"

"As long as her drug levels come down, she should be fine. The biggest concern right now is potential bleeding from the aspirin she took." Mitch didn't lie to them. Trina's chances were good.

He wasn't as convinced the same held true for the baby.

Unsure of what else he could say to make them feel better, he hesitated. Dana put her arm around Trina's mother. His brows rose in surprise when the woman turned and gave her a hug.

"I hope she wakes up soon."

"She will, don't worry. Just keep talking to her. Often patients can still hear, even if they can't respond."

Trina's mother did as Dana suggested. Dana was a great nurse, but the tears spiking her lashes confirmed she cared almost a little too much.

But Mitch couldn't find fault, not when he longed for some of Dana's caring concern for himself.

Trina's baby was still alive.

Dana continued to care for her two patients, Trina and Jessica, but the news about Trina's baby made her feel light-hearted and relieved. Trina's parents had gotten weepy all over again when they'd learned the news, even though the OB/GYN physicians had been cautiously optimistic.

"Miscarriages are not uncommon in the first trimester," they'd warned. "Everything seems fine now, but we'll need to watch her closely over the next few weeks."

Trina was only ten weeks pregnant and Dana wondered if desperation over discovering the news had led to the overdose or if there was something more. Either way, she hoped Trina would seek help. The girl had a long road ahead of her and her life would be forever changed from this point forward. At least her parents seemed supportive and willing to help her through this.

She couldn't help comparing Trina's father to hers. The envelope he'd given her was still at home on her kitchen table, unopened. When she'd left for work, she'd planned on tossing it in the garbage without reading it when she returned home.

Now she wasn't so sure.

Not that she expected her father's letter to describe the depth of feeling Trina's father displayed, but she was struck by the way Trina's parents supported their daughter despite everything that happened. They kept reminding Trina how much they loved her and how everything would work out fine.

Dana found herself believing them.

Believing her own father wasn't nearly as easy. Why had he left her all those years ago? Did he deserve another chance? She honestly didn't know.

Jessica's condition was pretty much unchanged, and she learned from the day-shift nurse that Jessica had reached a higher level on the transplant list. She hoped that meant good news for Jessica and her two kids. So far, she hadn't seen Wendy and Chad visiting and hoped they were spending more time with their father.

At dinnertime, she headed down to the cafeteria to grab a salad. When she stood in line to pay, Mitch came up behind her.

"I'll take care of both meals," he told the cashier.

"You don't have to buy me dinner," she protested.

"I know, but I'd like to." Mitch followed her to a nearby table. "Do you mind if I sit with you?"

"No, I don't mind." Talking to Mitch would help keep her mind off her father. "But why are you here so late?"

"What do you mean?" He raised a brow as he took a bite of his hamburger.

"You do realize none of the other intensivists work this late unless they have a really good reason," Dana pointed out. She stabbed at her salad, thinking Mitch's juicy burger looked very good. "Isn't that why you have residents? So they can stay and do the work while you go home?"

"I like to teach," he answered seriously, between bites. "And I care about the patients."

She didn't doubt him. His concern for Trina had been very real. He'd been especially happy to see Trina's drug levels were starting to come down, if slowly.

"You're just afraid your residents are going to do something wrong," she teased as she snitched one of his fries.

"Nah, they're doing pretty good." Mitch shoved the fries toward her in silent invitation to have more. Sitting here with him, sharing his food, seemed strange, yet at the same time comfortable. As if she didn't have to be someone she wasn't in his company.

"I noticed you seemed upset when you came to work," Mitch said. "Everything all right?"

"Sure." She shrugged, amazed at his perceptiveness. How did he pick up on the slightest change in her moods? When he frowned at her in disbelief, she amended, "Actually, I was a little upset. My father showed up on my doorstep right before I was due to come to work." She grinned wryly. "For a moment I thought he was a door-to-door salesman and almost shut the door in his face."

"What happened?" Mitch's keen gaze probed hers.

"Nothing. He gave me a letter, asked me to read it, then left." Dana tried to make light of the situation, but at the time her body had gone numb. She still had trouble believing the whole episode hasn't been some strange dream.

"What did the letter say?"

"I don't know." Dana stole another fry. "I didn't read it."

Mitch sucked in a quick breath. "You threw it away?"

"No, but that was my plan." She sighed, and picked at her salad. "Except now I'm not sure what do to."

Mitch didn't respond and she looked up, wondering what he was thinking. The first time he'd learned about her father he'd urged her to give her father another chance. Did he still feel the same way? Dana wasn't sure she wanted more advice from Mitch—he couldn't understand how hurt she'd been when her father had left all those years ago. For a long time she'd wondered if she'd done something really bad to make him go away. Nightmares had plagued her, and she'd often woken her mother up in the middle of the night. When she'd finally explained about the nightmares, her mother had confessed that the real reason her father had left had had nothing to do with Dana. It had been because he hadn't loved *her* anymore.

Dana couldn't quite understand why her father had stopped loving her, too, but at least the nightmares had faded. Still, once again she wondered why he had bothered to seek her out now after all these years.

"So what do you think?" Dana couldn't stand the silence any more. "Should I read his letter?"

Mitch glanced at her. "I think if you couldn't throw the letter away, your heart is already giving you the answer."

She rolled her eyes at his serious tone. "I was running late for work."

"I'm sure it's hard for you to understand what happened all those years ago." Mitch leaned forward, his expression earnest. "But only your father knows his true reasons for leaving. Can you live with yourself if you don't at least try to understand them?"

"I don't know." Dana abandoned her salad and propped her chin in her hand. Talking to Mitch was surprisingly easy. Being friends wasn't so bad after all. "I honestly haven't thought about him much over the past few years."

"You're afraid." He nodded. "I understand."

"Not afraid, exactly." Dana didn't like to think fear was the overriding emotion here. "More wary."

"Maybe you shouldn't be alone when you read it."

Dana knew Serena would support her if she asked, but Serena was off over Christmas because she and Grant were going to his parents' for the holiday. Caryn, too, would have been there for her, but Caryn was going through tough times of her own and Dana didn't want to add to them. "I'll be fine."

Mitch reached across the table and took her hand in his. "I know it's at times like this you probably miss your mom the most. I'll sit with you while you read the letter if you like."

Stunned by his offer, she didn't know what to say.

"I went through some difficult times a while back, and I should have found someone to talk to, but I didn't." Mitch held her gaze with his. "I don't want you to make the same mistake." He touched her hand lightly. "Your choice, Dana. But just know I'm here for you."

CHAPTER NINE

"THANKS." DANA WAS touched by Mitch's sincerity. It had been a long time since a man had cared enough to lend her a comforting shoulder to lean on. Most of her former relationships hadn't lasted that long. "I might take you up on your offer."

"Good." Mitch flashed her a reassuring grin. "I'll stick around until you've finished your shift, then follow you home. Unless you'd rather wait until tomorrow?"

"I'm not sure I can wait that long," Dana confessed. Then a twinge of guilt tightened her chest. "Although I know you have to be here at the hospital again early in the morning. Why don't we wait? I'm sure it won't kill me to hold off reading it for a few days."

"No, we'll do this tonight. I think the minute you see that letter sitting there, you'll want to read it." He glanced at his watch. "I'll grab a quick nap while you finish your shift. How about we meet up in the unit at eleven?"

She hesitated, knowing she was taking advantage of him yet at the same time unable to let him off the hook. She nodded slowly. "All right. If you're sure you don't mind."

"No problem." He eyed her half-eaten salad. "Are you finished? You didn't eat much."

"Only half your fries," she countered with an exasperated sigh. "Besides, I need to get back up to the unit."

Mitch stood, then took both of their trays and carried them over to the tray line. "Page me if I'm not up on the unit by eleven."

"Sure." Dana felt warm and tingly when he gave her hand a gentle squeeze. She suspected he might have kissed her if they hadn't been standing in front of the diners in the cafeteria, and she was surprised by how badly she wanted him to kiss her again. "See you later, then."

They parted, and Dana returned to the ICU alone. There was plenty of work to keep her busy, but time seemed to crawl by, especially when she stared at the clock every five minutes.

Jessica was tired and somewhat lethargic. Dana would have been concerned except that her oxygenation saturation on the bi-pap mask was holding at 92 percent. After verifying she was really all right, she moved on to Trina.

Her parents held vigil at the bedside. Not until right at the end of Dana's shift did Trina open her eyes and look directly at her parents seated beside her bed. Immediately, the young girl's eyes filled with tears.

"Don't cry," her mother begged, crying herself. "Everything is going to be all right."

Trina's father stood and took Trina's hand. "The baby is fine." His voice broke and he had to clear his throat before he could continue. "And so are you. We're sorry we didn't know how depressed you were, but your mother is right—we're here and everything is going to be fine. We'll get through this together."

Trina blinked away her tears and nodded. She couldn't talk because of the breathing tube in her throat and Dana stepped forward.

"As soon as her drug levels come back at a less than critical level, we won't have to give any more charcoal and then we can take that breathing tube out," she explained. "Hopefully by the morning."

Trina frowned, shook her head and pointed to the tube, indicating she didn't want to wait that long for it to come out. Dana could understand—she knew the breathing tube was hardly comfortable. But neither was getting more charcoal.

"I'm sorry, but we can't take the tube out yet." Even though she wanted to make Trina feel better, there were some things that couldn't be rushed. "We need to protect your airway, should the drug levels change for the worse."

"We understand." Trina's father spoke up. "Thanks for letting us know."

Dana documented another set of vital signs on Trina's clipboard, then glanced at Trina's parents. "Do you need anything else? I have to check on my other patient."

"No, but thanks." Dana's mother looked relieved. "We'll stay the night if you don't mind."

"We don't allow cots in the ICU, but you're

welcome to stay in the family center." Dana smiled at them both. "You might want to take turns, so you get at least a little sleep. I'll let the family center know your plans."

She made the necessary calls, then went to make one last check on Jessica before it was time to give report. Jessica was resting comfortably, so Dana quickly noted her vital signs, then slipped back out of the room without waking her.

Mitch hadn't shown up by the time she'd finished report, so she paged him. Within a few minutes he called back. "I'm on my way," he promised.

She waited for him outside the unit, her stomach in knots. Now that it was nearly time for her to go home and read her father's letter, she felt inexplicably apprehensive. Maybe she didn't want to read the letter after all. Maybe she should just tell Mitch she'd changed her mind. She could wait a few days for Serena to return.

"Hi, Dana." Mitch greeted her as he stepped around the corner. "How was the rest of your shift?"

"Good. Trina woke up about an hour ago." She pushed her doubts away and turned down the hall toward the doorway leading out to the parking garage.

"Great news. I bet her parents are relieved." Mitch fell into step beside her.

"Did you take a nap?" she asked. He did look refreshed and she caught a whiff of his woodsy aftershave.

"Yeah. As a resident, I learned to grab sleep when I could." He held the door open for her and a blast of cold air hit her in the face. "Where are you parked?"

"Over there." She gestured to the slot where she'd left her car.

"Oh, I see it. And my car is on the lower level. Wait for me out by the exit and I'll follow you home."

She did as he asked. When she saw Mitch's headlights in her rear-view mirror, she headed home, thankful that the snow had stopped, at least momentarily. So far the winter weather had been mild, just a few inches of snow here and there, and she found herself hoping for snow at Christmas.

The thought of Christmas brought her back to the holidays and the promise she'd made to her mother.

What would her mother have thought of her father's unexpected arrival? If her mother were still alive, would she encourage Dana to read his letter? Her mother hadn't carried a grudge against her father—in fact, she hadn't really talked about him at all.

The ride home wasn't long, and when Dana pulled into her garage, Mitch parked outside and met her at the door. Having him over at such a late hour made her feel slightly wicked.

"Are you all right?" he asked.

She opened the door. "I guess so."

"Nice place." Mitch's admiring glance warmed her heart. "Did you live here with your mother?"

She nodded and tossed her coat over a kitchen chair. "I lived on my own for a number of years, then moved back after my mother was diagnosed with cancer."

"I see." Mitch took his coat off, too, and nodded at the envelope lying in the center of the table. "Is that the letter?"

"Would you like something to drink?" She rubbed her hands together, avoiding the letter for the moment. "I could go for some blistering-hot coffee."

"Sounds good." Mitch took their coats to the closet, then sat across from her at the table. Once she'd finished preparing the coffee, she brought two steaming mugs to the table.

Mitch sipped his without comment as she picked up the letter, staring at it for a moment.

"Your choice, Dana," he reminded her.

He was right. It was her choice and she didn't think she could live with herself if she ignored her father's letter. After taking a deep breath, she slid her nail beneath the flap and opened the envelope. Two sheets of paper slid out. She unfolded them and began to read.

Dear Dana,

Your mother sent me a note just before last Christmas, asking me to get in touch with you. I know there's a chance you may never read this letter, but I hope you will. If not now, then maybe someday you'll take the time to read this.

I'd like to ask for your forgiveness for leaving you and your mother. I know I don't deserve anything from you, but I'm asking anyway.

The divorce was my fault. I take full blame for the destruction of my marriage. Your mother told me I had a drinking problem, but I refused to believe her. Not even the night I picked you up from the sitter and nearly crashed did I believe I had an issue with drinking. But that was the night your mother gave me an ultimatum: stop drinking and get help, or leave.

I left.

I'd like to tell you how much I regret my decision, but I didn't, at least not right away. My righteous anger carried me through many years. Until the night almost two years ago when I ended up in the hospital with acute pancreatitis. I lost over a month of my life, most of the time spent in the ICU. I don't remember much, which is probably a good thing. Even when I was finally released from the hospital, my kidneys suffered severe damage, resulting in the need for dialysis three times a week.

Once I realized I did have a severe drinking problem, it was too late. I'd already lost you and your mother. I did get help and have been alcohol-free since coming off dialysis nine months ago. I would have returned sooner if I could have. I only wish there was a way for me to go back and change the mistakes from the past. Your mother was right. You were much better off without me.

I know I don't deserve a second chance, but I want you to know how sorry I am and how much I love you. I'm very proud of the wonderful person you've become. The patients in your care are truly blessed.

Sincerely,

Brian Whitney, your father

Her chest tight, Dana lifted her gaze to Mitch. His eyes, full of compassion, were glued to hers. Wordlessly, he stood and came around toward her.

"Come here." He took her into his arms and she leaned gratefully against his warm strength.

"Thanks. You were right, I'm glad I didn't read this while I was here alone." Her voice was muffled against his shirt. While she still regretted the years her father had stayed away, she found some solace in knowing he'd cared.

"Any time." Mitch rested his cheek against the top of her head and stroked a hand down her back. There was nothing sexual in his embrace, but her skin tingled down the length of her spine where he touched her. She tried to curb her rioting emotions. "I'm here for as long as you want me to be."

Like forever? She shook off the unrealistic expectation and closed her eyes, breathing deeply, filling her head with his wonderfully addictive scent. As much as she wanted to hate her father for his weakness, as a nurse she knew alcoholism was a disease. And while she wondered how he could walk away without even trying to keep in touch, she also knew things might have been worse if he had stayed.

At least her father had loved her. Maybe she wasn't completely unlovable after all.

"Do you want to talk about it?" Mitch asked in a low tone.

She shook her head. Right now, it was enough to know her father loved her. And she didn't want to think about the past, preferring to be submersed in the present. Being held by Mitch felt so good, so right, she didn't want him to ever let go. Lifting her head, she moved just enough to press a thank-you kiss against the side of his neck, the only area she could reach without pulling out of his arms.

When she kissed him, he sucked in a quick breath and every muscle in his body went tense. A tingly awareness coursed through her. Curious, she experimented again, pressing her mouth against his skin and tracing the surface with her tongue for a quick taste. His arms tightened, bringing her firmly against his hard length, changing the embrace from one of comfort to something far more urgent.

"Dana," he growled low in his throat, burying his face in her hair. "You'd better tell me to leave."

"I can't." Letting him go was the furthest thing from her mind. Although she wished they weren't standing in the center of her kitchen. Her bedroom was too far away, but the living-room sofa was much closer. Pushing the collar of his shirt out of her way, she explored the taut skin of his chest with her mouth.

Mitch slid his hand beneath her hair and brushed his thumb along the side of her jaw, urging her mouth up toward his. He claimed her mouth, lighting her soul with the depth of his kiss. The fierce intensity of his tongue moving with hers sent a surge of longing rocketing through her. She melted against him, the thin fabric of her scrubs a negligible barrier to his hard length.

In a quick movement he backed her up against the

kitchen table. His hands palmed her bottom and eased her hips up onto the smooth surface, then nudged her legs apart to fit against her more fully. When she gasped and hung on, he trailed a string of kisses down along her jaw.

"Dana, you're driving me crazy," he murmured between kisses. "I've wanted you from the moment I first saw you in the cafeteria."

She moistened her lips with her tongue, trying to think through the sensual haze. Mitch was always so kind and considerate. This new nearly out of control side of him sent her senses reeling. "I want you, too."

He lifted his head, staring down at her and breathing heavily. A haze of passion clouded his eyes. "If this is too fast, we can stop. I didn't come here for this."

Fast? Laughter bubbled in the back of her throat. If he left her now, she'd have to hurt him. Never had anyone wanted her like this before. She was eager to relish the sensation. She wrapped her arms around his neck and her legs around his waist, pressing the juncture of her thighs against him. "Stay."

He groaned again and took her mouth in another deep kiss. His taste was intoxicating and addictive—the more he kissed her the more she wanted. She wasn't sure how, but he managed to slip her scrub top up and over her head, tossing the garment on the floor.

When he gazed at her breasts revealed in the skimpy lace bra, she felt beautiful. Sexy. Desirable for the first time in forever. Eager to see him, too, she eased away to help with his clothing. He wore a long-sleeved shirt with a long row of infuriating buttons. When she couldn't get them open fast enough, he used one hand to hold her close while working the buttons with the other.

Soon additional articles of clothing littered the kitchen floor. She wanted to suggest they find her bedroom, but couldn't quite think of a delicate way to broach the subject.

"Mitch?" She hated the uncertainty in her tone.

"What is it?" He sensed her confusion and quickly tipped her head up to meet his gaze. "Have you changed your mind?"

"No." Dear God, no. She still wanted him, more than she would have thought possible. Her few previous sexual encounters had been simple, pleasant. Nothing nearly this wanton or thrilling. But as much as she liked the out-of-control feeling, the kitchen table wasn't very comfortable. "The table is cold and hard on my behind," she confessed.

He blinked, then started to laugh, a deep belly laugh she couldn't ever remember having heard from him before. She smiled, then began to laugh, too. They both laughed harder and harder until tears sprang to her eyes.

Mitch's pager went off.

His laugh turned into a groan, and he reached for his discarded pants to find the device. When he read the message, his expression turned grave.

"What is it?" She asked with a sinking feeling the news wouldn't be good.

"Trina's bleeding." His voice echoed with remorse. "Dana, I'm sorry."

She forced a smile, her laughter dissolving quickly into

regret. This was what happened when you became emotionally involved with a physician. "No problem. I understand." And she did. "I hope Trina isn't losing her baby."

"I hope so, too." Mitch bent and quickly rummaged through the clothes lying around the floor. He picked up her scrub top and helped her put it back on. "I can't believe I'm helping cover up this amazing body of yours."

She smiled at the honest frustration in his tone. "Me neither." He was being awfully nice, not leaving her sitting on the kitchen table, bare bottom and all. In fact, he made sure she had all her clothes back on before he found the rest of his.

When they were fully clothed again, he reached for his coat. "I really wish I didn't have to leave you like this, Dana."

The real concern in his eyes eased the awkwardness of the situation. "I know."

"We'll get together again soon." He bent to capture her mouth with his. "I'll call you tomorrow."

"Bye, Mitch." She walked him to the door, then stood and watched as he strode back out to his car, knowing things had somehow changed between them. Not just because they'd almost taken their relationship to an intimate level.

But because she'd just surrendered her heart.

CHAPTER TEN

MITCH OPENED HIS eyes, disoriented by the complete blackness surrounding him. Where was the sunlight? For a moment he thought he'd fallen back into that dark pit of despair after Jason's death, then he remembered.

He'd spent the night in one of the hospital on-call rooms after leaving Dana for the emergency in the ICU. There were no windows in the small resident call rooms.

Fumbling for the light switch on the lamp on the bedside table, he remembered the events from the night before with sudden clarity. Those magical moments in Dana's kitchen when he'd almost taken her like some horny teenager on the kitchen table. He should have been horrified by his actions, but instead his lower body stirred at the memory.

Dana was the first woman he'd cared about in a long time. And he couldn't make himself regret the time he'd spent with her. She'd needed someone after reading the letter from her estranged father and he had been glad to help.

Glancing at his watch, he realized the time was close

to eight. He needed to get back up to the ICU as soon as possible. He headed to the shower in the call room's tiny adjoining bathroom. His patients were waiting, specifically Trina.

The sixteen-year-old girl had lost her baby. The aspirin she'd ingested had been enough to prolong her clotting time and once the bleeding in her uterus had started, there had been no way to stop it.

Scrubbing his face in the shower, he tried to remember things like this happened for a reason, but he empathized with Trina and her parents. He knew first-hand how helpless he'd felt after Jason's death. He'd missed Dana when dealing with Trina and her family. Their overwhelming grief had reminded him what it had felt like to lose Jason. He'd been more than tempted to seek out Dana afterwards, only the knowledge she was sleeping preventing him from going over to wake her up.

To finish what they'd started.

After finishing his shower, Mitch yanked on a pair of scrubs in lieu of donning the same clothes he'd worn last night. He headed over to grab a bagel from the hospital cafeteria, washing it down with lukewarm coffee, before making his way up to the ICU.

"Sorry I'm late." He addressed his team of residents, who'd gathered behind the nurses' station. "Let's make rounds."

Quizzing the residents on various aspects of patient care took his mind off Dana. He led the team to Trina's bedside and asked the resident, Dr. Samuel, about Trina's latest aspirin level and hematocrit.

"Ah, her aspirin level is 20.2 and her hematocrit is 29.7."

"Do you recommend giving additional blood transfusions?" He asked the resident.

"Yes, one unit of packed red blood cells."

"No more blood yet." Mitch corrected. "She's young, healthy and there is always a risk with a blood transfusion. I think for now we should hold off and watch her."

The resident nodded. "Yes, sir."

"Is her aspirin level low enough for her to be transferred to the floor?" Mitch asked, putting the resident on the spot once again.

A few of the residents exchanged glances, as if trying to figure out what he wanted to hear. Finally Dr. Samuels shook his head. "No, her aspirin level should be lower than 15 to be considered safe enough to transfer out."

"Very good." Mitch glanced at Trina's chart. "What has the OB/GYN team said about her miscarriage?"

"They haven't been around yet this morning, but last night their opinion was that her high ASA levels caused the miscarriage."

Mitch silently agreed, although he'd like to be able to tell Trina and her parents something different. The guilt of this would sit with her for the rest of her life, too much of a burden for someone so young. Making a mental note to contact Social Services for psych support after discharge, he moved on to the next patient.

He finished rounds with Jessica. In her room, he was struck by her pale skin and wan smile.

"How are you feeling, Jessica?" he asked with concern.

"Weak," she admitted. "Like I...can't catch my...breath."

Mitch gazed at the information on her clipboard. Her oxygen saturation was hanging in the low 90s but he was troubled by her apparent listlessness. Her oxygenation would suffer with the smallest exertion. She wasn't running a fever, thank goodness, and he made a mental note to double-check her chest X-ray from earlier that morning to make sure she didn't have the beginnings of pneumonia. "I think we need to increase your Romadylin infusion."

"All right."

Her unenthusiastic response gave him pause. Was she getting depressed? Maybe antidepressants were in order. "Did your family come in to see you last evening?"

"No...they're coming...today."

"Good." Maybe seeing her kids would help lift her spirits. He wrote the order for the increase in her Romadylin infusion, then went out to find the nurse. He inwardly groaned when he saw Therese was assigned to Jessica. She stood outside another patient's room, jotting notes on a clipboard.

"Therese, I'd like you to increase Jessica's Romadylin drip."

She didn't spare him a glance. "Fine."

Ouch. Apparently Therese hadn't been as drunk as he'd thought if she could still hold a grudge. He waited a moment and when she didn't move, he grew impatient. "Now, if you don't mind," he snapped.

"I'm in the middle of something." She continued writing on the clipboard, impervious to his urgency. "Leave the order. I'll get to it soon."

Her couldn't-care-less attitude set his teeth on edge. If he knew the intricacies of the CAD pump, he'd change the infusion rate himself, but the CAD pumps were very different from a regular IV pump and he didn't want to risk making a mistake. He spun around, intent on finding the pharmacist on duty, when he caught sight of Caryn. Grateful to see a friendly face, he approached her.

"Caryn? Will you do me a favor?" He handed over the order. "Increase Jessica Kincade's Romadylin for me?"

"Sure." She took the order and headed straight for Jessica's room. If Caryn noticed Therese wasn't too busy to do the task herself, she didn't comment. Since the increase was slight, it would take a couple of hours to see the effect on Jessica's pulmonary status, which was why he'd been impatient to increase the dose right away.

Mitch finished with the team right before lunch. He figured he'd grab something to eat, then give Dana a call.

Since he couldn't use his cellphone in the ICU, he went to the lobby after he'd finished eating to call her. Caryn had given him Dana's phone number, although he'd had to endure the knowing glint in her eye when he'd asked for it.

Her phone rang several times, then the answering-machine kicked in.

"Dana, it's a little after noon and I'm calling to see how you're doing." He paused, feeling stupid. Now what? "Give me a call on my cellphone when you have a minute." He rattled off the number. "Thanks. Bye."

He snapped his phone shut and strode back toward the ICU. Was Dana avoiding him on purpose? He couldn't imagine why but he also couldn't claim secret insights into a woman's psyche either. Leaving her when they'd been close to consummating their relationship hadn't been easy.

Inside the ICU he decided to check on Jessica. His steps slowed when he saw Dana standing in Jessica's doorway, wearing soft, worn jeans and a bright red and green Christmas sweater. For a moment he was thrilled she'd come to see him, but then took another step into Jessica's room and warned himself to get a grip. Dana was the sort of nurse who cared enough to check on her patients, even when she wasn't working.

"Dana!" A young voice called her name seconds before Wendy launched herself at Dana who laughingly caught the child against her.

"Hi, Wendy." She pressed a quick kiss on the top of Wendy's red hair then lifted her gaze to Chad. "Hi, Chad. How are you? Win your hockey game?"

"Yeah." The boy shuffled his feet, obviously uncomfortable with his sister's display of affection.

Undeterred by his lack of enthusiasm, Dana put her hand on his shoulder and squeezed gently. "Glad to hear it." The boy didn't pull away from her touch and when she smiled at Chad he amazingly returned it with a shy one of his own. She hugged Wendy to her side and at that moment, seeing Dana with Jessica's kids drove a glaring truth through Mitch's heart.

Dana was meant to be a mother. To have a family.

The soles of his feet congealed to the floor as he absorbed the picture they made. One in which he was certain he couldn't share. Because no matter how he wished otherwise, the fear of making the same mistakes he'd made in the past returned full force.

His marriage hadn't been able to withstand the tragedy of losing Jason. Dana wasn't Gwen, but he accepted at least half the blame for their marriage falling apart. He'd buried himself in work, rather than trying to work through things with Gwen. And Gwen had chosen to start over, with someone new.

He wasn't sure he could do the same. Neither was he sure he could trust himself to react any differently if something like that happened again.

He couldn't trust himself not to hurt Dana.

Dana hid the depth of her concern behind a facade of cheerfulness. Jessica looked worse than ever, more lethargic and listless than the night before. Only a few days left until Christmas and right now Dana doubted Jessica would make it to see the New Year, unless she was lucky enough to receive a double lung transplant.

A desolate sadness washed over her. She couldn't stand knowing Jessica might die over the holiday, the same way her mother had. Poor Wendy and Chad. There had to be something she could do to bring a little holiday cheer to their lives.

Turning away, she glanced over her shoulder and saw Mitch staring at her from across the unit, his mouth tight and unsmiling. She was taken aback by his uncharacteristic expression, then realized he must be worried she'd attached more importance to their intimacy last night than the situation had warranted. Did he think she'd turn into some sort of clinging vine, tracking him down here while he was working?

The idea made her feel slightly sick to her stomach. No surprise to figure out he wasn't as emotionally involved in whatever had transpired between them as she was.

Surprisingly, he didn't avoid her though, but came forward to Jessica's room. His facial features relaxed a bit as he approached. His gaze skittered away from hers, but he greeted them all easily enough.

"Hi Wendy and Chad. Dana." He stood with his hands thrust deep into his pockets. "I'm glad you're here. Isn't it great to have your family here to see you, Jessica?"

Jessica nodded. Dana refrained from rolling her eyes. Quite a turn-around from a few weeks ago when he hadn't wanted the kids exposed to the ICU environment, she thought.

"Dr. Reynolds." Dana purposefully used the formality. "I see you've increased her Romadylin."

He nodded, his expression turning serious. "Yes, first thing this morning. How do you feel, Jessica? Breathing any better?"

The patient nodded, although in Dana's opinion Jessica didn't look any better. "Yes, a little."

"Good. I think we'll probably get another chest X-ray in a little while just to make sure we're not missing anything else." Mitch nodded at the group. "Any other questions, let me know."

"Thanks Dr. Reynolds." Jessica gave him a fragile smile that nearly broke Dana's heart.

He glanced at her. "Ah, Dana? Do you have a minute?"

"Sure." She followed him out of Jessica's room. But he didn't go far. He dropped his voice so the information wouldn't carry.

"I wanted to let you know, Trina lost her baby."

She sucked in a quick breath. "Oh, no."

"She and her parents took the news pretty hard." Mitch's expression betrayed a similar sadness. "I thought you should know, in case you'd planned to visit with her, too."

Since she had been planning to do just that, she nodded, appreciating his foresight. "Yes, thanks. I'm glad you told me. Did she say why she took the overdose of pills?"

"Sort of. She admitted to feeling depressed for months because of not having any close friends. Her parents had commented on her slipping grades. She got in with a bad crowd at school, then became pregnant. I guess she felt as if everything in her life was going wrong. Classic clinical depression, but very treatable with the right medication."

"I'm glad."

Mitch hesitated as if he wanted to say more, then took a step back. "There's a patient on the floor I have to go evaluate for a possible transfer to the ICU, so I'll see you later."

Dana watched him leave then headed back into

Jessica's room to chat with the kids. Last night she'd worried that the bleeding Trina had been experiencing hadn't been good news. This result was probably better for Trina in the long run—sixteen was too young to shoulder the responsibility of raising a child. Still, she ached for Trina. At least her parents were supportive and with the help of her family Trina would get through this.

"Have you ever seen the play, *The Christmas Story?*" Wendy was asking her mother. "Cindy told me it was really cool."

A shadow crossed Jessica's features. "No, I haven't seen it, honey. But maybe once I'm better we can go."

"That would be fun." Wendy didn't dwell on the play, but Dana knew the play wouldn't continue to run after Christmas.

"If I could get tickets, maybe we could all go." The instant Dana had uttered the invitation, she grew excited at the prospect. She and her mother had often gone to see Christmas plays. She liked the idea of helping Jessica's family experience this one Christmas tradition.

Wendy's eyes widened. "Even Mommy?"

"Of course. Well, I'd have to get permission from Dr. Reynolds first," she quickly amended. "But if we were only gone for a few hours and came right back here, maybe he'd let us go." As she spoke, she warmed to the idea. "We can take a wheelchair and a portable oxygen tank. Since I'm trained to take care of Romadylin and bi-pap masks, I can't see why a short field trip would be a problem."

"Really?" Wendy's face lit up with excitement. "Wow, that would be so cool."

"Are you sure you're up to this, Mom?" Chad, the responsible one, asked doubtfully. "We can wait until you're better if you'd rather."

"I'd like…to see the play." Jessica nodded. "If Dana…would come with us."

"I'll clear it with Mitch, er, Dr. Reynolds when he gets back," Dana promised. She glanced at her watch. "First I have to see if there are even tickets available. I'll get back in touch with you as soon as I know for sure."

She left the unit without talking to Mitch as he hadn't returned from seeing his patient on the floor. Although her mind was already formulating her argument as to why he should let her do this, she missed the closeness they'd shared last night.

If she was honest, she had intended to use her visit with Jessica as an opportunity to see Mitch again. She truly hadn't minded that he'd been forced to leave to deal with Trina's miscarriage. Yet after his strange reaction to her unexpected arrival on the unit, maybe it was better to give him the space he so obviously needed.

At home later on, when she listened to her messages on the answering-machine, her pulse spiked at the sound of Mitch's husky voice. A tiny flicker of hope flared deep in her heart. He'd actually called to check on her.

When she listened to the message a second time, she realized he'd called just after noon, but she'd gotten to the hospital about that same time. So the moment he'd looked at her with barely disguised antipathy had been after he'd left the message.

What had transpired in the meantime?

She had no way of knowing. With a quick movement she hit the erase key and deleted the message. She didn't know what had happened to change his mind but, as much as she would have liked to spend her day off with him, she didn't return his call.

Dana set the phone down after almost two hours of planning. She'd finally gotten tickets, travel arrangements and equipment organized in order to take Jessica and her kids to the play that evening.

The only downside was that Mitch had insisted on going with them. As much as she'd tried to convince him his presence was unnecessary, he'd insisted on coming or he wouldn't allow Jessica to leave the unit.

Left with no choice, she'd given in gracefully.

Just as she was about to head to her room to change, the phone rang again. Figuring the caller had to be Mitch, she muttered something unkind under her breath and picked up the phone. "Now what? I told you I have everything covered. You have to trust me on this, Mitch."

There was a long pause, then a deep male voice asked, "Dana? How are you?"

It took her a moment to recognize the voice of her father. She was glad he wasn't there to see her blush. "Sorry, I thought you were someone else."

"That's all right. I just called to see how you were doing." He cleared his throat. "I'm, uh, sorry to bother you."

"You're not," she lied. Actually, Brian was bothering her, had cost her many hours of sleep since he'd given her the letter. But after reading his words and seeing events through his eyes, she couldn't seem to hold onto her anger. "But I am getting ready to go see a play with a patient and her family. Maybe we can talk another time?"

"Yes. Any time you're free would be great." Her father sounded more than a little enthusiastic. "I'll leave my number."

Dana dutifully wrote his number down, then said goodbye. Long after she'd hung up she stared at it.

Talk about a total switch. After years of indifference toward her father, she was actually looking forward to talking to him again. And to think her mother had sent him a note some time last year, before she'd passed away.

"Dana, promise you'll always hold the joy of Christmas in your heart." Her mother had gripped her hand on Christmas Eve. "Promise me," she'd reiterated when Dana hadn't answered right away.

"I promise." Dana had choked back her tears.

"Ah, Dana. Don't cry." Her mother, weak from disease, had smiled. "I've had a wonderful life. My only regret is leaving you alone."

Dana had bent her head to hide her tears and when she'd looked up again, her mother's eyes had slid closed.

Then she had gone.

Her mother hadn't pined after her father when he'd left, at least not that Dana could tell. She wished her mother was here now, to talk through her confused feelings for Mitch.

Dana had no idea what she was going to do about the man she'd given her heart to.

CHAPTER ELEVEN

MITCH COULDN'T BELIEVE he'd let Dana talk him into this cockamamie idea of taking Jessica and her two kids to see some Christmas play in downtown Milwaukee. He'd tried to get her to drop the whole idea, but when Dana latched onto something, he discovered there was no way to convince her to let go.

The thought of spending the whole evening with her was pure torture. At least they wouldn't be alone. In fact, the only reason he'd finally given in and given the go-ahead had been because Jessica hadn't looked very well and he hadn't been able to ignore the bad feeling in his gut that told him her days were numbered if she didn't get a transplant soon.

Trust kind-hearted Dana to figure out the same thing for herself. He thought it was great, the way she wanted to give the family something fun to remember during the holiday. But he hadn't been able to shake his bad feeling about Jessica's condition, so he'd spent an hour getting someone else to cover his call for the evening, so he could go, too.

As he met up with Dana outside Jessica's room, he glanced around in amazement. She'd gotten Jessica into a high-backed wheelchair and was hooking up the bi-pap mask and machine to a portable oxygen tank mounted to the back of the chair. Jessica was securely tucked into the chair with pillows for maximum comfort, covered up to her chin with a warm blanket. There was only one tiny problem that he could see. "Uh, Dana? How are we going to get the wheelchair transported to the theater?"

"I have a transport van waiting for us downstairs, courtesy of Horizon Homecare." Dana finished setting up the oxygen tank and stepped back to give the connections one last look. "They were happy to give us a special discounted holiday rate."

He imagined there was more to that story, but didn't ask in front of Jessica's kids. "Sounds good. We probably need some emergency supplies, too, just in case."

"I already have everything we need." Dana held up a small red plastic box. "I have intubation supplies in here, and the respiratory therapy department is letting us borrow their portable suction machine. I also have first-line emergency meds, the same variety we take with us on road trips."

He had to grin. The ICU nurses described taking critically ill patients to Radiology for tests and procedures as road trips. Having coded his share of patients in Radiology, he knew the nurses preferred to be prepared.

Dana certainly had everything under control for this extended road trip.

"I guess we have everything we need, then." He gestured to the door. "Let's go."

They were a funny-looking entourage as they headed down to the main lobby. Little Wendy was so excited she skipped alongside her mother's wheelchair, chatting a mile a minute about nothing in particular.

Chad was quiet, but Mitch could see the boy shared a bit of his sister's excitement, especially when he saw the oversized van outside. "Hey, check this out, Mom. It's practically a limousine for patients."

Jessica smiled and nodded. The driver of the van came around and greeted Dana with such familiarity Mitch figured they had to be friends away from work. Must be how she'd gotten her special holiday discount. After opening the van doors, the driver took a remote control and unfolded the wheelchair lift.

Dana helped get Jessica's chair loaded onto the lift and secured in the back of the van without any difficulty. Then the rest of them climbed in behind her, leaving Mitch to sit up front with the driver.

Mitch listened to the kids and Dana as they headed downtown. There was a rather lively discussion about the merits of *A Christmas Carol* as compared to *The Christmas Story.* Since he'd never seen the latter, he didn't have much to contribute to the conversation.

They arrived at the theater in record time. He took some of the heavy supplies from Dana while Chad steered his mother's wheelchair. Dana led the way to their seats, located in the back of the theater where Jessica's wheelchair wouldn't block anyone's view.

The four of them sat in the last row, with Jessica in her high-backed wheelchair directly behind them. Mitch found himself seated beside Chad, with Dana on the opposite side next to Wendy, reminding him of the way his parents had purposefully seated his brothers and sisters between them.

The perfect family.

Guilt stabbed his heart when he realized he hadn't seen his family since his divorce. They'd been close, but their constant sympathy had gotten to the point where he'd felt he needed to escape. He knew they blamed him for the divorce because he'd dealt with his grief by burying himself in his work, neglecting Gwen. He hadn't been able to explain that Gwen had avoided him as much as he'd avoided her.

He wondered what his brothers and sisters were doing now. Spending time with their own families and his parents, no doubt, going through the last-minute rush of preparing for the usual Christmas celebration.

He needed to call them. Although he was scheduled to work through the holiday, he should at least make contact with his parents. Maybe he could squeeze a quick trip in to see them after he had finished working his stint in the ICU.

Mitch didn't pay attention to the play at first. Instead, he listened to Jessica's audible breathing from behind them. Every few minutes he glanced back to make sure she was doing all right, only to find her attention was riveted on the action unfolding on stage. Soon the story sucked him in. Hearing Wendy and Chad giggle along with Jessica's soft laugh, muffled behind her bi-pap mask, warmed his heart.

Dana's instincts had been right when she'd arranged this little outing.

When the play ended, he rose to his feet like all the others, applauding the actors, who returned to the stage to take their final bow. The young child actors were the best and even Chad let out a loud whistle when the young teenage heroine of the play took her bow.

"That was so good." Dana surreptitiously wiped her damp eyes. "I'm glad we came."

He was too choked up himself to do anything but nod in agreement.

"Me, too!" Wendy hopped up and down from one leg to the other. "Mommy, did you like the play?"

"Very much." Despite the bright excitement in her eyes, Jessica's voice was faint, causing Mitch to glance at her with concern. They gathered around Jessica's wheelchair, waiting for the crowds of people to diminish before heading out to where the van waited.

"We'd better go." Mitch exchanged a long, knowing look with Dana. She picked up on his concern and quickly nodded in agreement.

"All right, Chad, you get to steer your mother's chair." Dana picked up the portable suction machine case and slung it over her shoulder.

Mitch tried to take it from her, but she shook her head and handed him the red box instead. They took the elevator to the main lobby and headed outside.

"Look, Mommy, it's snowing!" Big fat flakes were

falling from the sky. Wendy lifted her face to the sky and stuck out her tongue for a taste.

The snow must have started a while ago because a fresh layer of glistening white snow covered every surface, including the horses that stood attached to the carriages along the side of the street.

Wendy saw the horse and carriage rides at the same moment Mitch did. "Look at the horses, Mommy." She frowned. "They shouldn't make the horses carry people for rides in the snow. They're gonna get cold."

"They have thick winter coats, Wen." Chad rolled his eyes. "The horses will be fine."

Mitch half expected Wendy to ask for a ride, but she didn't. Dana was busy loading Jessica's wheelchair in the van, and soon they were all packed in and ready to go.

Jessica's breathing seemed to echo loudly in the tight confines of the van as the driver pulled out onto the snow-covered streets. Mitch glanced back and saw Dana was just as worried.

"We'll be back at the hospital in no time," Dana reassured Jessica. "Do you need to be suctioned?"

"No. I'm...fine." Jessica responded.

Mitch didn't like the way Jessica looked, and the last thing he wanted to do was to intubate her in front of her kids. Despite the rapt expression on Jessica's face as she'd watched the play, he hoped this trip hadn't been too much for her.

Mitch glanced back at Jessica, who sat back in her wheelchair with her eyes closed. Dana stayed close, her fingers resting along Jessica's wrist, monitoring her pulse.

He leaned close to the van driver. "Whatever you do, don't slide off the road, but get us back to the hospital as quickly as possible," he murmured.

Silently, he prayed. *Hang on for a little while longer, Jessica.*

Dana held her breath during the entire trip back to Trinity Medical Center. If anything happened to Jessica *en route*, she'd never forgive herself.

The way Mitch kept glancing back at them told her he was concerned, too. Jessica's features had grown even more pale, and her breathing was slightly irregular.

Dana tightened her grip on the emergency box containing the intubation equipment and mentally counted Jessica's heart rate again. Why had she thought this would be a good idea? What if this trip ended up costing Jessica her life?

Dana swallowed hard and sought to get a grip on her rioting emotions. Jessica hadn't exactly been the epitome of health today—hadn't Mitch increased her Romadylin infusion that morning? The trip to the theater had been made with the least amount of stress to Jessica as possible. Her breathing could have changed for the worse while Jessica had been lying in ICU.

All of which might be true, but Dana had a hard time making herself believe it.

Finally her friend Jake, the van driver, pulled up to the front doors of Trinity Medical Center. Dana had never been so glad to see the brightly lit hospital in her entire life. Moving quickly, she jumped out and waited impatiently as the lift lowered Jessica's wheelchair to the ground.

"Thanks so much, Jake." Dana said, quickly taking possession of Jessica's wheelchair. "I'll settle up with you later."

Jake simply nodded, understanding the undertone of urgency that hovered beneath her cheerfulness. "See you later, Dana. Merry Christmas, everyone," he added as she pushed Jessica's wheelchair inside.

They didn't run back up to the ICU, but if Dana could have made the elevator move a little faster, she would have. Soon they piled back into Jessica's empty room.

"Chad, would you and Wendy wait outside while I transfer your mother back into bed?" Dana asked, moving the wheelchair into position. "Should only take a few minutes."

"Sure." Chad gave her a quick look, as if picking up on her worry, but ushered his sister out of the room.

Dana lowered the back of Jessica's wheelchair and then poked her head out the door. "I need lifting help in here."

"Did you have fun?" Amber, the nurse assigned to Jessica on second shift in Dana's place asked as she entered the room. "Was the play good?"

"The play was great." Dana couldn't bring herself to look at Mitch who stood in his smart slacks and sweater, watching their patient like a hawk. Was he blaming her for Jessica's turn for the worse? She couldn't blame him if he did. "But help me get Jessica back into bed. Her breathing sounds labored."

They made the transfer easily enough, with the help of Mitch's strong arms and the sliding board. Once Jessica was safely back in bed, Dana reconnected her to the heart monitor above her bed.

Mitch took out his stethoscope and listened to Jessica's lungs. Dana got rid of the rest of the equipment, then waited for him to finish his exam.

"I think we're going to have to intubate her," he murmured half under his breath. "We can hold off for as long as possible, but her lungs are definitely worse."

"My fault." Dana gripped one of Jessica's side rails, her knuckles white. "I shouldn't have taken her out into the cold."

"You're smart enough to know the cold air didn't cause this, Dana." Mitch glanced down at Jessica, who was still lying with her eyes closed, as if to concentrate on her breathing. "Jessica? Can you hear me?"

She nodded, then opened her eyes and turned towards them. The silent plea was almost Dana's undoing. "I can't breathe."

"I know." Mitch placed a hand on her arm. "We've maxed the dose of your Romadylin infusion, Jessica. The only thing left is to do an elective intubation to hold you over until you can get a double lung transplant."

Jessica gave a resigned nod. "Do it, then."

Dana had to turn away and blink back sudden tears. Jessica's silent bravery made her want to cry. She quickly gathered the supplies they'd taken on the trip so Mitch could perform the intubation.

Amber called for respiratory therapy assistance and

they brought up the ventilator. Because Amber was the nurse on duty while Dana was technically off duty, Amber gave Jessica the medication to relax her for the procedure.

Mitch placed the breathing tube without difficulty, then ordered the proper ventilator settings. Once Jessica was safely breathing along with the ventilator, she stepped out to the waiting room to inform Wendy and Chad.

"Hey, guys." She tried to smile but her face felt as if it might crack with the effort. "Dr. Reynolds needed to give your mom a breathing tube to help her breathing. She's doing fine," she added quickly when their eyes widened in alarm. "And the breathing tube is going to help rest her lungs so she doesn't have to work so hard."

"When she doesn't need the tube any more, will Dr. Reynolds take it back out?" Chad asked.

"Yes." Dana didn't add that the likelihood of that was slim. "He won't keep the tube in unless she needs it."

"Can she still talk to us?" Wendy asked, her lower lip quivering.

"No, honey, I'm afraid not." Dana gathered the girl close. "But she's awake and is ready to see you. Don't be afraid of the ventilator—just remember that it's helping her breathe."

The kids wore solemn expressions as she guided them back to Jessica's bedside. Jessica opened her eyes to see them, but when her lips moved and she couldn't talk, Wendy burst into tears.

"Shh, it's OK." Helplessly, Dana held her close. "Your mom can still hear you."

"We're here for you, Mom." Chad stepped forward, taking his mother's hand in his. Wendy calmed down a bit when she saw her brother's steady attitude.

Jessica made a gesture with her right hand and Dana quickly recognized what she meant. "Just a minute," she promised, then dashed out of the room to get a piece of paper and a clipboard.

When she returned, she held the clipboard up so Jessica could write. After a few minutes Dana smiled and held up the clipboard so Chad and Wendy could see.

Jessica had drawn a large heart with the words "I love you Chad and Wendy" written in large block letters inside it. When the kids saw the note, they responded instantly to the crude form of communication.

"We love you, too, Mommy." Wendy brushed aside her tears. "Can I write you a note, too?"

When Jessica nodded, Wendy took another piece of paper and proceeded to do just that. Even Chad didn't bother to point out that Jessica didn't need a note because she could hear them.

After a few minutes of writing notes back and forth, Jessica looked tired, so Dana encouraged the kids to say goodbye. Then Jessica wrote one last note, but handed the clipboard to Dana.

Please call Rick and let him know. The kids need their father.

Dana nodded. "I will."

As it turned out, Rick wasn't home so Dana left a message. Not until after Jessica's mother had picked up the kids did she seek out Mitch.

He was in the unit, but came over when she walked in. "Do you have a minute?" she asked.

"Sure." He turned and walked into the empty nurses' lounge.

"I wanted to apologize." Dana couldn't bear to look him in the eye, so she kept her gaze trained on the Christmas tree she'd decorated. "I never should have put Jessica's life in danger."

"You didn't. Dana, look at me."

She reluctantly raised her eyes to his.

"You have to trust me on this. You didn't cause Jessica's need to be intubated. Heck, she'd been looking worse all day. In fact, I think you timed it perfectly. If you'd waited another day, it would have been too late to go to the play."

As nice as he was being, Dana couldn't let herself off the hook. "How do you know the stress wasn't too much for her?"

"Dana, did you hear her laughing during the play?" Mitch asked. When she nodded, he continued, "Did she sound stressed?"

"No, but dragging her outside, in the snow and cold, couldn't have been good for her."

"You had her bundled up to her nose and she was outside for barely five minutes to get her into and out of the van." Mitch reached out to capture her hands in his. "Don't do this to yourself. You did a wonderful thing for that family, giving them a memory they can hold on to forever."

Dana stared at their clasped hands, blinking back tears. "She isn't going to last much longer, is she?"

"No. I'm afraid not." He tugged her close and all her previous doubts evaporated as she gladly stepped into the warm circle of his arms.

"Will she get a transplant soon?" Dana asked, even though she knew it was a stupid question. Mitch couldn't control when organs would become available for transplant.

"I hope so." Mitch's breath tickled her ear. "Ironically enough, intubating her probably moved her up the list. She has blood type A, which is common enough for her to qualify for a transplant sooner than most."

Dana nodded, knowing he was right. Her own problems paled in significance when she thought about Jessica and her fight for her life, so she squared her shoulders and pulled out of Mitch's embrace.

"Thanks, I needed a hug." She smiled, to let him know she wasn't attaching special significance to their brief embrace. She tugged at the collar of her turtleneck sweater. "I'd better get home so I can get some sleep. I have to work the next few days in a row."

Mitch nodded, then put out a hand to stop her from brushing past him. "Stay with me."

"What?" She couldn't have heard him right then realized he might be afraid of talking to Jessica's kids alone. "Don't worry, Chad and Wendy have gone home with their grandmother."

"Stay," he repeated. "I don't think you should be alone right now." When she raised a brow, he quickly added, "All right, I don't want to be alone either. I want to be with you."

She shouldn't. Spending more time with Mitch would only mean more heartache. But the intense expression in his eyes was enough to make her resolve waver. "I thought you were on call?"

"I am, but I don't need to stay here in the hospital. I thought we could go back to my place—it's only a mile from here." Mitch's expression was full of hope.

"All right." She was surprised when the words popped out of her mouth. So much for her sense of self-preservation. "At least for a while."

She couldn't stay away from him.

CHAPTER TWELVE

MITCH WAS TEMPTED to pull Dana back into his arms for a quick kiss, but didn't want her to think all he wanted was sex, although his body ached to be with her. He hadn't lied when he'd told her he didn't want to be alone. And with everything that had transpired during the evening, he didn't think she should be alone either. If this really was her last day off before Christmas, he didn't want to waste a second of the free time they'd have together.

The fact that he'd failed in his resolve to stay away from her didn't escape his notice.

He strove to keep his tone light. "OK, we have two choices. We can either sit in one of the call rooms to talk, or you can let me take you back to my place. I don't know about you, but I'm hungry. I have some leftover Cavatelli to share."

"More Italian?" She laughed. "Why not? Now that you mention it, I'm hungry, too. I was so busy making sure I had everything organized for the trip to the play that I forgot to eat."

"Great." Mitch was more than a little relieved she wasn't put off by his suggestion. He would keep things light and friendly between them if it killed him. He turned toward the door. "Are you parked in the parking garage?"

"Yes. I'll follow you."

"Sure. Unless you'd rather I gave you a lift?" Mitch was hoping she'd planned to stay late at his place, like all night.

She hesitated. "I'd rather drive, I guess."

Hiding his disappointment, he nodded. "Sounds good."

His condo wasn't far from the hospital, so they arrived at his place in less than ten minutes. He indicated she should park alongside him and they walked up to his door together.

The front door opened into his living room and her gaze went straight to the bookcases that flanked the fireplace. "Oh!" she gasped, her eyes wide. "You have so many books."

"Here, let me take your coat." He shrugged out of his own first, then helped take off her long wool coat. She looked adorable, her sleek black slacks and plum turtleneck sweater emphasizing her slender frame. "I'll be right back."

When he returned from stashing the coats in his closet, she was still standing before his bookcases as if starstruck. "You're welcome to take anything you'd like to read," he offered, pleased she shared his love for books.

"Thanks so much." She cocked her head and grinned. "So, you're like a part-time librarian then?"

"Not exactly. I'm making an exception, just for you."

"I'm honored." She placed a hand over her heart and fluttered her lashes.

With a laugh he gestured toward the fireplace. "First I'll start a fire, then we can eat."

She watched as he quickly stacked the wood for a fire. The newspaper below the logs crackled as the flames caught. He glanced over his shoulder at her and the delighted expression on her face was enough to make him curl his fingers into his fists. Slow, he reminded himself. They were taking things slow. He stood and brushed the debris from his pants. "Have a seat. I'll heat up the Cavatelli and bring it in here for us."

"I don't even know what Cavatelli is, but it sounds good." Instead of sitting down, Dana followed him into the kitchen. "Is there something I can do to help?"

Kiss me. "Uh, no, just make yourself comfortable." Keeping his hands occupied with food was probably a good thing, or he'd have been tempted to toss her down to the carpet in front of his fireplace and have his way with her.

Dana helped him carry their plates to the living room so they could watch the fire as they ate. Cavatelli was his favorite food, but he could hardly taste the delicious pasta, his body was so tense with longing. From the very beginning he'd known Dana was a nurturer, but he hadn't known how badly he'd wanted someone to nurture him.

Not just anyone. Dana.

He tried to keep the conversation light as they ate. But all too soon Dana glanced around the room with her brow pulled into a deep frown. "I have to admit, I'm disappointed."

His gut twisted. Hadn't she liked his books? His fireplace? Him? "With what?"

"No Christmas decorations." She gestured toward his fireplace. "That mantle is begging for stockings to be hung by the chimney. And where is your tree? Heck, I'd settle for a wreath. The area above the fireplace is perfect for a wreath."

His appetite vanished and he lowered his fork to his plate. "Guilty as charged. I've lost interest in Christmas, I guess."

Her gaze dropped to her plate. She was too astute for her own good and knew he held back the truth. "I see."

Mitch set his half-eaten food aside, realizing he wasn't being fair. Dana deserved the truth, but he was loath to bare the dark secrets of his past.

Although he respected her enough to know she needed to be told. Everything. Starting with the horrible way he'd lost his son, followed by his failure as a husband.

"That's all right. You don't have to explain," Dana said in a low voice, sensing his dilemma.

He took a deep breath and let it out slowly. "Yes, I do."

Dana knew she was pushing with her need to know the mysteries of his past, but she couldn't seem to curb her desperate curiosity. The void where his holiday spirit should have been bothered her more than she wanted to admit. Granted, he'd come to the unit Christmas party, but even then they'd ditched the others a few minutes after he'd arrived.

His words proved Christmas had once meant something to him.

I've lost interest in Christmas.

Mitch stood up, picked up their plates and carried them into the kitchen. When he came back, he added another log to the fire and took a seat beside her on the sofa, close enough to touch but keeping that inch of distance between them.

"I was married for three years." He didn't look at her as he spoke, but kept his gaze trained on the flames dancing along the log. "My wife wasn't in medicine, but she seemed understanding of the demands of my career."

Dana nodded, waiting for him to continue.

"We'd talked about having kids but she wanted us to wait until I'd finished my fellowship. I think she was under the impression my hours would become more reasonable then."

Dana winced, remembering the way their evening had been interrupted the other night. "Wrong. But if she loved you, I'm sure she understood."

"I was surprised and thrilled when Gwen told me she was pregnant." Mitch stared down at his hands, as if the past was almost too difficult to talk about. "We were the closest we'd ever been during those months of her pregnancy. Our son, Jason, was born on September eighteenth."

At first she frowned, because he'd told her he didn't have children, then the tortured expression in his eyes confirmed her worst fears. She reached over, took his hand in hers. His fingers were cold to the touch and she wrapped both of her hands around his, trying to infuse him with her warmth. "I bet he was adorable."

"He was. His smile could light up your soul." He momentarily closed his eyes. "He died on Christmas Eve."

She sucked in a quick breath. "No."

Mitch pulled his hand from hers and she could feel him emotionally pulling away, too. "Sudden infant death syndrome."

Dana couldn't imagine how awful it must have been to lose a child so abruptly. She swallowed hard. "I'm sorry, Mitch."

He nodded. "The worst part of all was that Gwen and I dealt with our grief in totally different ways. She threw herself into the effort to prevent SIDS. Joined the SIDS foundation, met with other parents who'd suffered similar losses. But I couldn't do it. I didn't want to dwell on the disease that stole my son's life. I buried myself in my work, which only caused a wider rift between us."

Her heart wept for him. How awful to lose your son and your wife at almost the same time. "You were hurting, too," she reminded him.

"Maybe. But so was Gwen. And I wasn't there for her."

"She wasn't there for you either."

He shrugged. "She found someone else through the SIDS foundation. They were married about six months ago and she's already expecting their first child." He shook his head in disbelief. "I can't believe she's brave enough to try again."

Because he wasn't? Dana had to bite her lip to keep from asking.

He finally brought his gaze up to hers. "I have to be honest with you, Dana. I'd made up my mind to stay out of relationships, but it hadn't worked. Because here I am, with you. Losing Jason felt like someone had ripped my heart out of my chest. For months I kept thinking I could hear him crying and would wake up from a sound sleep, only to realize he was gone."

Oh, Mitch. "I can't even imagine what you must have gone through," she murmured. She'd lost her father at a young age, but to lose a baby seemed so much worse.

"I still have some of this things, clothes, toys and a glass Christmas ornament with his name etched into it that I bought the week before he died. I haven't been able to bring myself to give them away."

"You will when you're ready." Dana didn't know what else to say. Jason would always be in Mitch's heart.

"Maybe. I know this isn't fair, dumping all this on you, Dana, but I thought you should know the truth."

The bruised expression in his eyes convinced her he was truly torn between the pain of the past and the hope of the future.

"Mitch." Dana put her arm around his shoulders and gave him a hug. "I'm here because I care about you. I'm glad you told me."

She didn't know what else to say. How did you help ease pain this deep? She kept her arm around him and rested her head on his shoulder. His story did help her to understand him a little better, but at the same time she knew he was also warning her away. He wasn't quite ready to start over again.

She swallowed hard. His warning had come just a little too late. She already cared about him. Too much.

"Enough rehashing the past." He cleared his throat and stood his back stiff and straight. "Thanks for sharing dinner with me. It's late, you probably need to get going."

She knew leaving would be the smart thing to do. But she couldn't do it, even to save herself from heartache and pain. She gave him a sad smile. "Are you kicking me out, Mitch? Because I'm not in a hurry to leave."

Startled, he shoved his hands in his pockets and glanced at her. "I don't want to hurt you."

"I'm responsible for my own emotions." She rose to her feet and came toward him. "If you'd really rather be alone, I'll go. All you have to do is say the word."

When she smoothed her hands over his chest, gently kneading his sculptured muscles beneath his sweater, he shook his head helplessly. "I can't. Heaven help you, Dana, I'm selfish enough that I won't ask you to leave."

"Good. I don't want to go." She pressed herself against him and tugged his head down to hers. She kissed him with all the warmth and healing she held in her heart, wanting nothing more than to help ease his pain.

He crushed her close, hauling her up against him and angled his head, deepening the kiss. The intensity of his desire made her want more.

The fire crackled and popped, sending a showering of sparks up the chimney. Impervious to the heat surrounding them, he lifted her up and gently set her on the sofa.

She'd intended to heal him, to infuse him with her love, but his kisses turned edgy, intense. The same sharp passion that had almost caused her to allow him to take her on the kitchen table clutched her again.

He drew her turtleneck sweater up and over her head and she arched her back when he lowered his mouth to her breast. Need spiraled through her and this time she prayed there wouldn't be any interruptions. Her fingers tried to peel his sweater away, but couldn't quite manage. He ripped the garment off, muttering, "Damn winter. Too many clothes."

Instead of answering, she pressed her mouth to the bare skin of his chest, licking, tasting. His skin was so hot it almost burned.

Soon the annoying barrier of their clothing melted away. Mitch took a moment to provide protection and then turned back to Dana. "Beautiful. You're so beautiful." Mitch kissed her everywhere—her breasts, her stomach and lower still. She tensed, then gave herself over to the sensation, her body shuddering in response.

"Beautiful," he whispered again, kissing his way back up her body to her breasts. "I could watch you do that all day."

As good as he'd made her feel, she wanted more. She wanted him.

He didn't make her wait.

"Mitch." He plunged deep, and she gasped his name. Mitch groaned low in his throat. For a moment he held himself still, not moving except for when he kissed her. "Please," she begged. "Don't stop."

"Never." He slid a hand beneath her hips to deepen the sensation, then began to move, slowly, gently at first, then with increasing urgency.

Dana didn't recognize herself, the way she greedily took as much as she gave, glorifying in the maelstrom of their desire.

When pleasure exploded, sweeping them both at the same time, one thought dominated all others.

She loved him.

Mitch woke slowly, one satiated muscle at a time. When he opened his eyes and saw Dana sleeping beside him, he was glad to realize he hadn't dreamed her. Those precious hours had been very real. With regret, he glanced at the clock. As much as he wanted to stay with her, to start this new day making love, he needed to get to the hospital to see his patients.

He dragged himself from bed, taking care not to wake her. Times like this made him wish he'd chosen to be a dentist. Even a Radiologist, didn't have to take call as much as he did.

But the notion was quickly superseded by thoughts of his patients. Jessica in particular. How had she fared during the night? He hadn't been paged, so he couldn't imagine she'd been anything but stable on the ventilator. And what about Trina? Chances were, her aspirin levels were probably low enough to warrant a transfer out of the ICU.

After showering and changing his clothes, he was ready to go. Tiptoeing back to where Dana still lay sleeping, he gazed down at her for a long moment. He was partially surprised to realize he didn't feel any panic or dread that he'd taken his relationship with Dana to a new level. Instead, he was forced to admit he liked the way she looked in his bed.

His family, especially his mother, would love her.

Mitch grinned and bent down, to press a feather-light kiss on her cheek. Dana stirred, murmured something unintelligible.

"Make yourself at home, sweetheart." He told her. "I'll call you later."

She nodded without opening her eyes, then buried her face into his pillow. He straightened, then turned to leave.

On the way to the hospital, he took out his cellphone and called his mother. There was no answer at home, so he left a message.

"Hi, it's Mitch. I just wanted to wish you a merry Christmas. I'm going to the hospital now, but I'll leave my home number in case you want to me call back later." He recited the number, paused, then added, "I miss you. There's so much we need to talk about, the past as well as the future. I have to work the holiday, but hope to make a trip back home soon. I love you."

He snapped his phone shut, feeling as if a weight had rolled off his shoulders. Light-hearted, he felt like laughing. Even the cloudy gray sky couldn't dim his happy mood.

No, nothing could bring him down. Not when he was busy making plans to have Dana meet his family.

CHAPTER THIRTEEN

DANA AWOKE TO find herself alone in Mitch's bedroom. Disappointed, she sat up, holding the sheet to her chin and looking for her clothes, only to remember they were probably still strewn about his living-room floor.

The memory of how they'd made love on the sofa in front of the fire made her blush. Of course, that had only been the beginning. An appetizer of a sort. He'd made the rest of the night a special five-course meal. Absolutely perfect. Except for waking up alone. With a frown, she thought she remembered Mitch giving her a kiss and telling her to make herself at home. Obviously he'd had to go in for rounds first thing this morning.

Awkwardly, she yanked the sheet from the bed and wrapped it around her torso, unable to bring herself to walk through the empty condo completely naked. Should she really stay until it was time to get ready for her shift? She felt funny being here without him. She found her clothes, then made her way to his bathroom.

Less than an hour later she rummaged in his fridge for something to eat. She found milk and eggs, but wasn't in the mood to cook, so she went through his cupboards until she found a box of cereal. After eating breakfast, she wandered back into his living room, drawn by his overflowing bookcase.

There were several Cavenaugh titles, but she was surprised to find Mitch's reading tastes varied from legal thrillers to horror to sci-fi and even a smattering of pure suspense. She found a suspense book she'd been dying to read and pulled it from the shelf. She built up a small mound of wood in his fireplace then lit a fire, taking his request to make herself at home literally. She curled up in a corner of his couch to read.

When the phone rang nearly an hour later, she hesitated. Not her house, not her phone. But had Mitch said something about calling her later? Hoping she was right, she set aside her book and hurried over to the phone.

"Hello?"

"Oh, dear," the female voice said. "I must have the wrong number. I'm looking for Mitch Reynolds."

"You don't have the wrong number," Dana quickly responded before the woman could hang up. "Mitch Reynolds is at the hospital. Do you want me to give him a message?"

There was a slight pause, then the woman answered. "Oh, yes. Please, tell him to call his mother, no matter how late he gets in. Is he all right? It's been so long since I've spoken to him, I just need to know he's all right."

Mitch's mother? For a moment Dana thought she couldn't possibly have heard right. Then her words sank in. "I'm a friend of his so I'll give him the message. He's fine. Er…how long has it been since you've talked?"

"Over a year." Mitch's mother sounded near to tears. "No one in the family has heard from him for so long. Please, ask him to call me back as soon as possible."

"I will." She forced the words past her constricted throat. Mitch had a family. The phone dropped from her numb fingers, hitting the counter with a clatter. Blindly, she grabbed for it. She couldn't fathom why he'd told her about losing his son and his divorce, yet not mentioned that he hadn't spoken to his family in a year.

She wrapped her arms around herself, suddenly cold.

Maybe he had a good reason. Not all families were nice and cozy, she knew, but his mother hadn't sounded like some horrific person. Heck, his mother hadn't even questioned the strange woman answering his phone. If her mother had called and a strange man had answered the phone, you could bet the guy would have been drilled non-stop for information.

A wave of nausea surged over her. She abruptly remembered how upset her last boyfriend had been to find out her mother had been sick because Dana hadn't shared that very personal part of herself with him. Now she knew what it felt like to be on the other side. Mitch had tried to warn her, but she hadn't listened. Mitch wasn't as engaged in the relationship as she was. He'd claimed he didn't want to hurt her, and her blithe response had been that she was responsible for her own feelings.

Well, she was. The feeling of her heart being ripped to shreds was a direct result of her actions. She'd made the decision to stay. To make love. Mitch had gone through a lot over the past two years—it wasn't his fault he wasn't ready for more.

She was fooling herself to think he might love her in return.

Dana let herself into the house she'd once shared with her mother. Memories flooded over her. She wished more than anything that her mother was there. She could have used her mother's sound logic and common-sense approach in talking about Mitch.

She had to go to work in four hours, but she didn't know how in the world she was going to face him.

Eyes burning with the need to cry, she stoically blinked back the tears and headed to the kitchen.

She picked up her father's phone number from where she'd left it on the counter and stared at it. Talking to Mitch's mother had made her realize she owed it to her father to at least talk to him.

After dialing her father's number, she held her breath, waiting. When he picked up, she sighed in relief.

"Hello?" his tone was wary.

"Hi, it's, uh, Dana." She swallowed hard. "So. How are you?"

"Dana. I'm so glad you called." He paused. "Do you have time for lunch today?"

"I'm sorry, I have to go to work soon. But maybe after the holidays we could find some time to get together."

"I'd like that." He sounded pleased.

"Great." Dana took the piece of paper with her

father's number on it and put it behind a magnet on her fridge so it wouldn't get lost. "Merry Christmas."

"Merry Christmas, Dana. We'll get together soon."

She couldn't bring herself to call him Dad, but hung up the phone feeling somehow at peace. She was finally ready to forgive him.

Now, if only she could learn to ignore the pain of a broken heart.

Mitch drove home for lunch through another inch of snow. The snow had been coming down on and off over the past few days. Not a blizzard, but steady. Luckily, the plows were able to keep up.

He stepped inside and was more than a little disappointed to discover his condo was empty. The half-open book on the sofa and the smoldering remains in the grate of the fireplace were proof Dana had stayed for a while, but although he searched around the sofa, his kitchen table, even the bedroom, he didn't find any sort of note.

He frowned. Why would she leave without a word? He opened his phone and checked again, but there were no new messages.

His appetite gone, he jammed his fingers through his hair. He tried to tell himself she'd just gone home for a change of clothing, but his instincts were clamoring loudly in his head. He'd picked up his phone to call her house when he saw it. She had left him a note after all.

Call your mother.

While he was happy his mother had returned his call,

he was puzzled by the underlying tone of Dana's note. It seemed terse. Angry.

Quickly, he dialed Dana's home number. The phone rang and rang, then her answering-machine came on. Forced to leave a message, he asked her to call him back, then hung up.

At least he'd see her at work later.

He debated calling his mother back, then decided to wait. He had been planning to surprise Dana by taking her home to meet his family. He'd been so confident he'd already booked airline tickets, but now he wondered if maybe she wouldn't appreciate him planning her days off.

Mulling over the best time to spring the tickets on her, he headed back to the hospital. Only two days before Christmas and for the first time in a long time he was actually looking forward to the holiday.

The afternoon dragged by slowly. On any other day he'd have been tempted to leave the ICU patients in the hands of his residents, but he wanted to wait until Dana arrived. Maybe they could have dinner together in the cafeteria again.

He stood and watched Dr. Andrea Drake, one of his residents, place a central venous catheter in their new patient, Mr. Grady. A gentleman in his sixties, Mr. Grady suffered from chronic congestive heart failure. Mitch had already ordered a Foley catheter and had given Mr. Grady Lasix to pull off the extra fluid in his lungs. But Mitch wanted the central venous catheter so they could keep an eye on his fluid status, because he also suspected Mr. Grady was malnourished and dehydrated.

When he was certain Andrea had successfully placed the catheter in Mr. Grady's subclavian vein, he headed over to the nurses' station. Dana was getting the rundown on the patients and didn't acknowledge him.

He waited patiently for her to finish. When she turned from the board he took his chance. "Hi. I missed you at noontime."

"Really?" Her cool tone sent warning tingles down his spine. "Did you return your mother's call?"

"Not yet." He wrinkled his brow. "Is something wrong?"

She stared at the assignment board, refusing to look at him. "I'm sorry, but I don't have time to chat. If you'll excuse me, I have work to do."

What had gone wrong? Mitch wanted to grab her arm and force her to talk to him, but she was right in that she was officially on duty. As much as he wanted to talk to her, this wasn't the time or place.

As he reviewed Mr. Grady's past medical history written up by the medical student, his mind wandered.

The note. It had all started with the note. Dana must have spoken to his mother. With a guilty rush he realized he'd never mentioned anything to her about his family. Was that why she was so angry?

Anxious for a chance to explain, he bided his time, waiting for Dana to take her dinner break. When the hour grew later, past eight o'clock, he wondered if she'd skipped dinner to avoid him.

He found her in Jessica's room. He watched her for a moment as she held Jessica's hand and spoke to her softly. "I just got off the phone with your mother. Chad and Wendy are doing great. They send their love."

Jessica clutched Dana's hand, her movements jerky, anxious.

Dana continued, "I called Rick last night, as you asked, but I don't know if he picked up the message or not."

Finally Jessica seemed to relax and closed her eyes. Dana turned to leave, but she halted abruptly when she saw Mitch standing in the doorway.

"Do you have a minute to take a break?"

She shook her head. "Nope. Too busy."

"You didn't take time for dinner," he pointed out. "Surely you have five minutes to spare?"

He got the sense she wanted to argue, but instead she nodded and headed for the nurses' lounge.

Thankfully it was empty. She stood with her arms crossed over her chest. "Have you called your mother yet?"

Why was she so concerned about his mother? "Dana, I'm not stupid. Obviously you're upset with me because I didn't tell you about my family. I'm sorry."

"Look, if you don't want to tell me about your family, that's your choice."

"It's not that I tried to keep some big secret, Dana." He was floundering a bit and tried to backtrack. "What do you want to know?"

She shrugged. "Whatever you want to tell me. Are you close to them?"

"Yes. We're very close." He tried to understand where she was going with this.

"Even though you haven't spoken to them for over a year?"

"Dana, it's not as bad as it sounds. Really, you're making a big deal out of nothing."

Dana glanced down at the floor, then shook her head. "I'm sorry, Mitch, but I think family is a big deal. It's part of who you are."

He didn't know what to say in his own defense. Because she was partially right. His family *was* a big part of his life. He'd just needed a break, a chance to start over.

A chance to heal.

"Your family seems very nice." Her tone softened just a little. "I hope things work out for you, truly. I'm not upset with you, I'm upset with myself. I just need a little time alone. Please, excuse me. I really do need to get back to work."

Helplessly, he stepped aside and watched her walk away.

He loved her, but the words stuck in his throat. Because loving Dana meant being in a relationship for the long haul. And not just the two of them, but a family. Children.

He waited for the panic to grab hold.

It didn't.

Instead, he realized how empty his life would be without Dana. Suddenly he understood why Gwen had been willing to take the risk.

Could he do this? Could he really commit to Dana?

Christmas was just around the corner. He prayed it wasn't too late to win her back.

* * *

Dana managed to avoid Mitch for the rest of her shift. Luckily, the time seemed to pass pretty quickly until it was time to head home.

Since she'd skipped dinner, she should have been hungry, but when she stared at the contents of her cabinets, she couldn't seem to dredge up any sort of appetite.

Closing her eyes, she rested her head against a cupboard, remembering the tortured expression in Mitch's eyes when he'd told her about his son's death. And how brave his ex-wife had been to try again.

Maybe she'd been too hard on him. Yet she also knew how much she loved him. If he wasn't ready for a relationship, she was probably better off without him.

Knowing that in her head didn't make the truth easier to bear in her heart. Giving up on thoughts of eating, she left the kitchen and headed up to her bedroom. But she wasn't tired, so she sat for a while, staring outside at the lightly falling snow.

One thought struck her as she got ready for bed. Her relationships in the past had never hurt as much as this recent situation with Mitch.

And for the first time she wondered how much of that was because she'd never let herself fall in love this deeply before.

Christmas Eve dawned with snow flurries. Dana tried to listen to Christmas tunes through her headset as she shoveled her driveway, but keeping her spirits up was difficult.

She made a couple of dozen Christmas cookies, finishing just an hour before she was scheduled to start work. She packed a bunch in a small tin, then headed out into the wintry cold.

The unit was busy when she arrived. Her heart sank because new patients would no doubt mean that Mitch would be hanging around in the ICU for most of her shift.

For once she wasn't in charge. But when she saw Amy come out of Jessica's room, she instantly knew something was wrong.

"Is Jessica all right?" She hurried over.

Amy shook her head. "She's worse. Barely responds to verbal commands. Her head is fine—we've already gone for a CT scan just to make sure. But she's giving up."

"She can't give up. Have her kids been in to see her?" Dana glanced into the room.

"Not yet, but they're on their way." Amy shrugged. "Maybe you'll have better luck getting through to her."

Dana fully intended to try.

The moment they sat down for report, the call came in from the Center for Organ Donations. "There's a donor up in the neuro ICU. Jessica Kincade is a match. Get her ready—she's going to the OR for a double lung transplant."

CHAPTER FOURTEEN

DANA RUSHED AROUND to make sure every detail was taken care of for Jessica's surgery. Although Jessica had been an patient in the ICU for the past week, there were still tubes of blood to draw for the lab, X-rays to take, and Mitch had requested a special catheter to be placed in her heart prior to going to the OR.

During the preparations Dana could only hope and pray the operation would be a success. Sad to think someone else had had to lose their life in order for this miracle to happen. Thank God for the wonderful family who'd turned tragedy into the gift of life.

She called Rick and left yet another message. Where was he anyway? He'd confessed to having a gambling problem, but she'd thought he'd changed his ways. For the kids' sake, she hoped he had.

She left a message for Jessica's mother too. In ten minutes, Jessica's mother arrived at the bedside with the kids.

Wendy and Chad looked scared to death and Dana couldn't blame them. But they both gave their mother a kiss before Dana wheeled Jessica away to the operating suite.

After she dropped Jessica off in the OR, she found the kids seated in the waiting room outside the ICU, gloomy expressions on their faces. She wondered where their grandmother was.

"Hey, no long faces. This is a miracle." Dana sat between them. "Your mom is getting a new set of lungs. What better Christmas present could you ask for?"

Wendy gave her a faint smile. "I know I asked for new lungs for my mommy." Her lower lip trembled. "But I changed my mind. I don't want her to get a new set of lungs. What if she dies?"

Dana had been tempted to kick the transplant surgeon for his rather thoughtless comment in front of the children, emphasizing how serious the surgery was and how Jessica's condition was critical. "Wendy, your mother needs this surgery to get better. The doctors have done lung transplants before very successfully. I'm sure your mom will come through the surgery just fine, you'll see."

"Do we have to go to the waiting room?" Chad asked.

She didn't want to send them there, so far away from the ICU. Especially since she had another patient to take care of. "Why don't you stay here for a little while and watch television?" There was no one else using the waiting area, and that way she could keep an eye on the kids herself. "I'll come back and let you know what's going on."

Chad and Wendy perked up at that.

"Is your grandmother coming back for you?" Dana asked.

"Yes. But I miss my daddy." Wendy looked as if she might cry again.

"I know you do." Dana wondered if their father had picked up her message yet.

Dana hurried back into the ICU to check on her patient. Mrs. Sanchez had gotten extremely sick from a bout of the flu but after two days in the ICU she seemed much better. Dana figured by the next day, the breathing tube should be able to come out and Mrs. Sanchez would be transferred to the floor.

Another nice Christmas present. Right up there with a new set of lungs.

Dana's shift seemed to crawl by, although she kept busy enough helping others. When she got a call from the operating room the only thing they'd tell her was that the surgery was going well and that they'd finished with the donor patient and had started on Jessica's transplant.

Dana hurried out to the waiting room to let the kids know. "Things are going very well," she informed them. Then she looked around with a frown. "Your grandmother isn't back yet?"

Chad frowned. "It's been snowing. Maybe she's stuck."

Trying to hide her concern, Dana murmured something that could be taken for agreement. Dana felt awful though about these two kids spending Christmas Eve alone in an ICU waiting room. She'd have to call Jessica's mother's house to see if she answered.

"Jingle bells!" Wendy exclaimed, jumping up from her seat.

What? Then Dana heard them, too, the distinct sound of jingling bells. When she glanced down the hall she saw a man dressed up as Santa, lugging a tree and a pack of presents as he strode toward them.

Wendy's eyes grew as round as saucers. "Look!"

Not until the Santa figure came closer did she recognize the man behind the beard.

Mitch.

As upset as she was with him, her heart did a funny little flip in her chest.

"Ho, ho, ho. Merry Christmas." He winked at Chad and Wendy. "Come on, kids, I need your help to decorate your mom's room so she'll see Christmas when she gets out of surgery."

Dana couldn't believe what she was hearing. "I'm not sure the hospital rules allow Christmas trees in patients' rooms."

"Rules, schmooles. It's Christmas." Mitch proceeded to head straight into the ICU and the two kids dutifully followed.

Surprised, Dana trailed after them. She wasn't really against the idea of decorating Jessica's room and anything that helped get the kids' minds off their mother's surgery was a good thing, in her opinion.

She listened to the laughter and giggles coming from Jessica's room as she took care of Mrs. Sanchez. The three of them, Mitch, Wendy and Chad, were decorating the tree with the ornaments Mitch had brought.

Before she could make the call to Jessica's mother's house, one of the ED nurses rang up. "Dana? I have a woman down here who claims she left two kids up in your waiting room."

"Yes. Is she all right?" Dana asked.

"Her car went into the ditch and they brought her here to so we could check her over. She's fine, though. We should be able to release her soon."

Dana sighed in relief. "Sounds good. Let her know the kids are doing fine up here."

A while later, she went in to see how they'd decorated the room. Mitch had several presents under the tree and he brightened when she walked in.

"There's a box under here with your name on it, Dana."

"Open it! Come on, open it!" Wendy jumped up and down with excitement.

"I'm working," she protested. Then she noticed several other boxes of a similar size under the tree for Wendy, Chad and even Mitch. Curious, she glanced at her gift. "I'll open mine if you open yours."

"All right." Mitch nodded. He pulled up several chairs for them to sit around the tree.

"Where's your beard?" she asked. He was still dressed in his red Santa suit, but there was no sign of the fluffy white beard.

"I took it off. Too itchy."

She grinned. "Yeah, I bet." When their gazes met in a moment of understanding, she tore her gaze away with an effort then carefully opened her present. Never had she been a tear-open-the-wrapping-to-get-to-the-gift-inside kind of person. She'd always taken her time, preserving the pretty paper, a hold-over from her mother's way of doing things.

"Takes you long enough," Chad complained.

"I'm getting it." Dana slid her thumb under the last piece of adhesive and drew out the box. Holding her breath, she opened it. Nestled inside the tissue paper was a beautiful hand-blown ornament in the shape of an angel. When she drew it out of the box, she saw that her mother's name was etched on the front of the angel's gown and the pink breast-cancer ribbon embedded into the glass beside her name. "Oh," she gasped, tears pricking her eyes. "It's beautiful."

Mitch handed each of the kids a similarly wrapped present. "In our family, Christmas is a time for remembering people." Mitch said as the kids tore open their own gifts. "We have Christmas ornaments made for all the people we love the most. Each year, we pull them out and hang them on the tree, and then we talk about our memories."

"That's a beautiful tradition," Dana murmured. Something her mother would have wholeheartedly embraced.

Chad and Wendy pulled out their ornaments from their respective boxes, a Christmas angel for their mother and one for their father.

"What about yours, Mitch?" Dana asked, once Wendy and Chad had oohed and aahed over their ornaments.

He took the box Chad handed him and opened it. Dana caught her breath when she saw he'd wrapped the ornament he'd bought for Jason two years ago. Jason's name was clearly etched on the front.

"This is just like a Christmas angel to me," Mitch said in a husky tone. "And I decided it was time to hang this ornament on a special Christmas tree, like this one."

Dana didn't know what to say when Mitch hung the ornament on the tree. She was proud of how he seemed to have made peace with his loss, but what exactly did that mean for the two of them? Would he risk having another family? She didn't know.

Yet his vulnerability only made her love him more.

There were other presents under the tree for Chad and Wendy, but neither of them seemed at all interested in the wrapped packages. Instead, they wanted to sit around and tell their Christmas angel stories.

They hadn't gotten very far when Caryn poked her head into the room. "Dana? The OR is on line one for you."

Jessica! Dana jumped up from her seat. "I'll be right back," she told them as she ran from the room.

She picked up the phone. "This is Dana."

"Jessica's just about finished with surgery. We're bringing her over in about ten minutes. She's relatively stable, for a double lung transplant."

"Great. We'll be ready." Dana replaced the phone and dashed back into the room. "Your mom is coming out of surgery in about ten minutes."

"Really?" Wendy clutched her mother's angel ornament to her chest. "Can we see her?"

"Of course you can, but first you'll have to give us a little time to get her settled in." Dana glanced over at

Mitch for help. He quickly gathered the presents under the tree and took charge.

"All right, we have to go back out to the waiting room for a little while. You don't want to get in the doctor's and nurses way, do you?" Mitch headed for the door. "How about you use this time to open your presents, hmm?"

When Wendy looked as if she might protest, Chad grabbed her hand. "Come on, Wendy, put your angel ornament on the tree so Mom can see it when she wakes up. Then let's go. The sooner we go, the sooner they can get Mom back in her room."

"All right." Reluctantly, Wendy did as she was told.

The kids followed Mitch out to the waiting room while Dana prepared the room for Jessica's arrival. After a silent internal debate, she left the tree where it was. The practice of placing fresh post-op transplant patients in isolation wasn't followed any more so, as far as she was concerned, the fake tree didn't pose a threat any more than the supplies in the room did.

Jessica was rolled through the doors and Dana was kept busy as she connected her to the monitors, checked her dressings, her vital signs and her ventilator settings. Her pulmonary status was the most important part of her post-operative care so Dana made sure she double-checked everything.

Mitch, as the intensivist on duty, came into the room a while later, dressed in his scrubs with his stethoscope around his neck. Dana appreciated that he'd taken the time to make sure the kids were settled in the waiting room first, especially since there wasn't much he could do for Jessica until the transplant surgeons were satisfied she wasn't bleeding and turned over her pulmonary care to him.

"I'm almost ready for the kids to come in," Dana murmured to him, when they were left alone in the room.

"Good." Mitch gave her a tired smile. "They'll be glad to see her, even if the effects of the anesthesia haven't quite worn off yet. Oh, and their grandmother is here now."

"Good. I'm happy to hear that," Dana confessed. "I'll go get them, then."

"I'll come with you." To her surprise, Mitch followed her out to the waiting area. When Dana started to explain things to the kids, Chad suddenly shouted, "Dad!"

Pausing in mid-sentence, Dana spun around. Sure enough, Rick came rushing in.

"I'm sorry. I've been plowing the roads all day and didn't get your message about the surgery until now." His eyes were a little wild. "How is she?"

"Fine. She's out of surgery and I was just explaining to the kids that she'll probably be out of it for a while yet."

"Thank God." Rick closed his eyes for a moment in relief. "I've been working a second job, plowing the streets for the city, to earn back the money I'd lost, to help prove to Jess I'm serious this time." He scrubbed a hand over his face. "But I wasn't planning on non-stop snow either. Especially at Christmas."

Dana wondered how the kids' grandmother would treat him, but she needn't have worried. The two adults greeted each other with wary politeness.

"I'll take all of you in to see her now, if you like."

The entire family eagerly followed her into the unit. Rick stood at his wife's bedside with his arms around each of his children, their grandmother close by. Dana thought it was too bad Jessica wasn't awake to appreciate the strength of her family's support.

Dana had taken a few steps backward, trying to edge out of the room, when Jessica opened her eyes and looked right at her mother, husband and children. Then her gaze shifted to the tree just behind them and Dana would swear her eyes crinkled in a smile before they drifted shut again.

After a few minutes Chad and Wendy explained to their dad and their grandmother about the Christmas angels, and Rick seemed impressed that he'd been included, too.

They weren't ready to leave until after Dana's shift was over. Wendy threw her arms around Mitch's waist to give him a hug. "This was the best Christmas ever."

Mitch stroked a hand over her bright hair. "I'm glad."

"I can't thank you enough for what you did for our family," Rick said to Dana and Mitch.

"You're welcome." Dana was so glad everything had worked out for the Kincade family, at least for the moment, barring any complications with Jessica's surgery.

Rick left with the kids, while Jessica's mother stayed with her daughter. Once they were alone, Mitch grasped Dana's arm. "Do you have a minute?"

She wanted to tell him she didn't, because being with him like this was too painful. Reluctantly, she followed him into the lounge area, which was glaringly empty now that Jessica's kids had left with their Christmas presents.

"Dana, I'd like a chance to explain." His earnest expression tore a ragged hole in her heart.

His discarded Santa suit in the corner reminded her of how far he'd come. The man who'd lost interest in Christmas had donned a Santa suit for the sake of his patient's children. How could she say no? "All right."

He hesitated, as if suddenly unsure of himself. The confident Dr. Mitch Reynolds was never uncertain. "I told you I was a mess after losing Jason, but you were right, I did leave out a part of the story. The reaction of my family. I'm sure they meant well, but I couldn't stand their pity. And somehow I convinced myself they blamed me for the divorce. Mostly because I'd blamed myself."

Dana frowned. "Divorce takes two."

Mitch lifted a shoulder. "I coped differently and neglected Gwen. Either way, the final result was that I took the chance to escape. Without considering how my family would feel."

"I see." She understood. Hadn't she used a similar approach in the past? How many times had her relationships with men fizzled out, without her realizing she had been half the problem? She'd held herself aloof, reserved, afraid to get too close for fear of getting hurt.

Even with Mitch.

"I did apologize to my mother this morning."

"I'm glad." Dana was horrified to realize she'd pulled away from Mitch during the time he'd needed her most. "I'm sorry. I had no right to judge you."

"Dana, don't apologize. You were the one who taught me to love again." Mitch pulled out a long envelope and handed it to her. "I'd already started to think about my family after I met you. These are the plane tickets I'd booked for us to go and see my family after the holidays."

Struck numb, she stared at the tickets. "You did?"

"Yes." He stepped closer, drawing her into his arms. "And I talked to Caryn about your schedule so I know you're off, but if the dates don't work for you we can change them." He lowered his voice. "One thing I'm completely sure of is that we can do anything, Dana, if we love each other enough."

"I don't know what to say." She looped her arms around his waist and lifted her gaze to his. "I'd convinced myself there was no hope for a future."

"I love you, Dana." He cupped her face with the palm of his hand. "You've brought me back to life, made me realize what I was missing. Without you I never would have learned to love again."

"I love you, too." Dana flashed a tremulous smile. "Thank you for the beautiful angel ornament."

"You're welcome. It's after midnight." He lowered his mouth to hers. "Merry Christmas, Dana."

"Merry Christmas, Mitch." When she rose up on tiptoe to return the kiss she had the sense her mother would have approved completely.

"Will you marry me?" he asked between kisses.

She smiled through tears of sheer happiness. Talk about the best Christmas present ever. "Yes."

"And have children with me?"

She gasped, and blinked to keep from crying again. "Yes. I'd love to have children with you. This will be the first of many Christmases we'll share together."

"Together," Mitch echoed. "I like the sound of that."

1106/03a

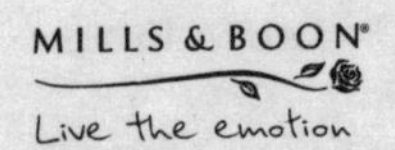

Medical romance™

THE MIDWIFE'S CHRISTMAS MIRACLE

by Sarah Morgan

It was a miracle he'd found her – freezing cold and alone in the snow. With nowhere else to go, Miranda Harding finds herself spending a magical Christmas Day with her disturbingly attractive rescuer, Jake. Consultant Jake Blackwell gets a shock the next day, when Miranda appears as the new midwife in his O&G department…and it is startlingly obvious she is six months pregnant!

ONE NIGHT TO WED *by Alison Roberts*

Dr Felicity Slade has come to the small coastal town of Morriston for a quieter life – and to distance herself from gorgeous paramedic Angus McBride. When Angus turns up as part of a medical response team her feelings are thrown into confusion. It becomes clear to Angus that this is his last chance – his one night to prove that he is the right man for Felicity…

A VERY SPECIAL PROPOSAL *by Josie Metcalfe*

Privileged doctor Amy Willmot has never forgotten her crush on Zachary Bowman – the boy with the worst reputation in town… Returning home, she cannot believe her eyes when she is introduced to the new A&E doctor – it's Zach! Can Amy persuade Zach to look past their backgrounds, and convince him that love really can conquer all?

On sale 1st December 2006

Available at WHSmith, Tesco, ASDA, Borders, Eason, Sainsbury's and most bookshops

www.millsandboon.co.uk

1106/082/MB060

There's always something special about a new Christmas story from Debbie Macomber!

Being stuck in a plane with pilot Oliver Hamilton during the festive season is not journalist Emma Collins' idea of fun.

But as time draws on it seems Oliver is not quite the Scrooge he appears…maybe there really *is* something special about Christmas!

On sale 3rd November 2006

www.millsandboon.co.uk